The Ambassador's Camel

Undiplomatic Tales of Embassy Life

David Holdsworth

With Drawings by Jean-H.

iUniverse, Inc.
Bloomington

iUniverse books may be ordered through booksellers or by contacting:

iUniverse
1663 Liberty Drive
Bloomington, IN 47403
www.iuniverse.com
1-800-Authors (1-800-288-4677)

ISBN: 978-1-4502-7663-4 (sc)
ISBN: 978-1-4502-7664-1 (hc)
ISBN: 978-1-4502-7665-8 (ebook)

Printed in the United States of America

iUniverse rev. date: 12/10/2010

For Nicole

Contents

Preface

I know what you will be doing a few pages from now. You will be trying to identify the diplomats and politicians in these pages and crying aloud, 'Aha, that's so-and-so! I know him or her.' Or, 'That's surely Minister So-and-so. I'd recognize him or her anywhere.' Alas, you will be wrong. The Bay of Bengal and Parliament Hill exist, but Bharalya and all the characters that inhabit this book are but figments of the author's fevered imagination.

You may also think writing is a solitary pursuit. That is true but not entirely. Jean-H. Guilmette, a fine artist and sculptor, agreed to do the drawings and commented on the characters and stories from the perspective of an illustrator. Johanna Read and Lea Stogdale, two wonderfully constructive and critical readers, ferreted out numerous weaknesses and errors and provided suggestions, which improved the book at every stage. And my spouse, Nicole, demonstrated limitless patience by suffering through every draft. Her unflagging encouragement combined with her honesty in telling the sometimes-difficult truth made it possible for these stories to see the light of day.

And finally, a tip of the hat to old LD, who showed the way.

Our Man in Bharalya

The foreign minister let out a resounding belch and pressed the button on his intercom. 'Send up Percy,' he barked to the quivering assistant outside his office. 'I have an offer he can't refuse.'

Now, what country was that visiting prime minister from at lunch today anyway, he wondered? *I never can remember those foreign names. He was so boring but at least the steak was good. I sure could use a quiet nap with my boots up on the desk right now. But I don't want to miss this meeting with that fancy-pants diplomat with the fancy-pants title: Senior Assistant Deputy Minister for Asia. No sir-ee.*

He licked his still-greasy lips with pleasure at the prospect of finally teaching Percy who was boss.

'What are you going to do to this guy, George?' asked Willy, his twenty-something chief of staff.

The minister snapped to attention. In his post-luncheon reverie, he had forgotten the presence of his political adviser. Willy was gazing through the grand floor-to-ceiling windows at the stunning view of the Ottawa River and the Gatineau Hills.

'Have you decided to tell him you're closing down that Asian embassy of his?'

'I'd like to close down the lot of them, for all the good they do me. The problem is, our oil and gas boys in Alberta tell me there's a big drilling contract coming up over there and they want me to avoid making the locals unhappy. No, unfortunately we'll have to keep the embassy open. Just for a little while longer. No, I have a better idea for Percy.'

'Smart move, boss. Never too early to think of financing your next election campaign.'

Ever since becoming Minister of Foreign Affairs of Canada three months ago, George Crowley had been at war with the senior diplomats of his governmental department. He didn't like them, he didn't understand them, and in any event, he was sure they were closet partisans of the Opposition.

He certainly never expected to be in Cabinet, especially on his maiden voyage to Ottawa. But in politics, timing and luck are often more powerful than ability. He was a self-made man who built up a small empire of used car dealerships in rural Manitoba. In his used-car world, he had been absolute monarch. He expected his employees to carry out orders without asking difficult questions. The professionals in his department, on the other hand, insisted it was their duty to advise him what he could or could not do.

'Percy and his gang of so-called experts even have the gall to oppose some of my ideas,' he grumbled. 'Willy, what was wrong with inviting all the Caribbean islands to join Canada? Canadians go there for holidays all the time; that way, they wouldn't need a passport. Or appointing my brother as ambassador to Italy? He loves pizza. Why not? Well, just let them try to stop me after they're posted to Siberia or Timbuktu.'

Just then the door opened and an immaculately dressed diplomat entered and crossed the thick carpet to greet him. 'Good afternoon, Minister,' he began, smiling pleasantly. 'I understand you wanted to see me.'

'I sure do, Percy. Let's sit over there. I have a very important matter to discuss with you.'

CR CR CR CR

As they moved toward the couch, Willy had a chance to compare the two men. They were roughly the same age, just over fifty, but otherwise could not have been more different.

George looks like a middle-aged prize fighter gone to seed, he thought. *Short, bald, and broad in the beam thanks to all those years noshing on hamburgers and fast food. Loves plaid shirts, suspenders, and most of all, straight talk. Successful businessman and big fundraiser for the Party. Only has a diploma from Manitoba Technical High but he made it in life anyway. Percy, on the other hand, looks and sounds like your model ambassador: tall, silver-haired, chiselled features, physically* fit. *Advanced degrees in economics and international affairs from Harvard and Oxford. Lots of international experience. And smart. Very smart.*

Those two are well matched, he decided. *This is going to be more a championship prize fight than a simple knockdown by the minister.*

From his ringside seat, he imagined an announcer stepping into the centre of a ring and calling out in a nasal twang:

> *In the* bluuuuuue *corner, The Minister, heavyweight, face like a punching bag, not too fast on his feet but has a powerful right hook and home advantage. Knows political power and is not afraid to use dirty tricks to win.*
>
> *In the* rrrrrrrrrrred *corner, The Diplomat, middleweight, twenty three years of senior jobs in Europe, Asia, and Ottawa, very fast on his feet and a survivor of a dozen ministers. The underdog but not to be counted out.*

The minister started by softening up his opponent. 'Great to see you, Perce,' he bellowed, slapping him on the back so hard that Willy thought a couple of ribs snapped. 'How's your lovely little wife, Jocelyne, doing?'

'Marilyn, sir.'

'Whatever.'

'Yes, sir.'

'So what are your plans for the future? I expect an experienced guy like you will want to go back abroad at some point. Am I right?'

'Haven't given the matter any real thought,' countered Percy noncommittally, feeling out his opponent's strategy.

The minister continued probing for a while. Then, when Percy dropped his guard for a second by talking about a job at the World Bank he'd like one day, George went for the sucker punch.

'The thing is,' he said, putting his hand on Percy's arm in what under other circumstances would be a gesture of camaraderie, 'there's a little country somewhere out there in Asia that's had a big oil find lately. Damned if I can remember the name, much less pronounce it. Starts with a B, I think. Butane? Banglydish? Something like that. Hell, Percy, do all those countries over there have to start with a B?'

'No, sir.'

'I met their ambassador with you one night at a reception. Talked about his days at McGill. A bit too smart for my taste though.'

'Bharalya, sir. It's a small country bordered by China, Myanmar, and Bangladesh. One end touches the Bay of Bengal, the other the Himalaya Mountains.'

'Could be. Anyway, we need someone there to help the drilling boys win some big contracts. The embassy's been without an ambassador for some time, I understand.'

Willy: *Point to The Minister for the element of surprise.*

Percy then danced backwards, deftly shifting into a classic bureaucratic defensive stance. He pretended to support the direction the minister wanted to take while simultaneously spelling out all the reasons why the minister should go in exactly the opposite direction.

'Yes, Minister,' he replied, bobbing and weaving. He had heard on the grapevine that the former Minister of the Environment had been looking for a soft landing after his defeat in the last election. 'You're absolutely right. Great idea. And I believe you and the Prime Minister already have a good candidate.'

Willy: *Throwing someone else to the lions. Point to The Diplomat. Throwing a politician to the lions, bonus point.*

'He had a better offer,' replied the minister, smoothly blocking the blow. 'A provincial judgeship. Anyway, his wife put her foot down when she found out there was no Holt Renfrew over there.'

Willy: *Two points to The Minister for deflecting opponent's punch.*

The minister did not tell Percy he had then offered the job to thirteen other people: defeated members of Parliament, party bagmen, a rich businessman looking for a new challenge, a well-known television personality, even a former wrestling star he met briefly at a Party fundraiser in his riding. To a man and woman, they turned down the dubious honour to serve their country in Bharalya's insalubrious climate.

Willy: *Point to The Minister for holding back key information.*

'In that case, Minister, I'd be happy to pull together a list of people from within the department who would like a shot at an ambassadorship. That will probably take some time but the acting ambassador can surely hold the fort until the next posting cycle.'

Willy: *Attempt to buy time. No points but a good try.*

'No, no, Perce,' George replied, moving in on his opponent. 'We'd like somebody senior, somebody really experienced. Right away. I think you'd make a perfect fit. You and your lovely wife Jocelyne.'

Willy: *Right hook to the chin. Three points for The Minister.*

'That's very flattering of you to think so,' responded Percy, dazed by the blow. Then shaking it off, he came back with a one-two combination of his own.

'But I thought you wanted to close that embassy. That's the message I've been getting from you for months. Anyway, I doubt the department could release me this year. You will remember I'm quarterbacking that Asian policy review your government promised in the Throne Speech. Changing horses in midstream could mean you as Minister of Foreign Affairs would miss the deadline the Prime Minister set you.'

Willy: *Three points to Percy for aligning political pain for the minister with his own personal interest.*

The minister was rocked back on his heels by that one but recovered quickly and moved in for the kill. 'Oh, I think the deputy minister can be persuaded to let you go. In fact, I've already had a personal word with her. I've promised her the job *she* wants next year if she finds a replacement for you. No one is indispensable, you know, Percy.'

Willy: *Knockout for The Minister. Match over.*

'You see, Percy,' said Willy, 'when policy and politics clash, politics always win.'

As Percy picked himself up, the minister, ever the used-car tycoon, gave him another bone-cracking slap on the back. 'A pleasure doing business with you, Perce,' he said with a broad grin. 'No hard feelings, eh?'

Kings and Dragons

Minister of Foreign Affairs

Communiqué

The Honourable George Crowley,

Minister of Foreign Affairs,

announced today the nomination of

Percival James Williamson

as Ambassador-designate of Canada

to the Kingdom of Bharalya.

Godfrey was amazed at the communiqué that flashed onto his computer screen. He had been consul for the past four years and acting Canadian ambassador to Bharalya for almost two. In absence of an ambassador, he had been in sole charge—an arrangement that suited him perfectly.

He quickly called the ambassador's personal secretary, known less than affectionately as The Dragon, into his inner office.

'Percy Williamson? Ambassador? Here?' he sputtered. 'That's impossible! He must have committed some terrible sin. My spies in personnel division assured me absolutely no one wanted to come to this forsaken place.'

'Now, now, Godfrey,' the Dragon soothed in a condescending tone. 'I know you are disappointed. I know you always wanted to be a full ambassador, just like your father, but it just isn't to be. Get over it … sir.'

The Dragon was a fiercely loyal, take-no-prisoners woman who had served and protected numerous ambassadors around the world for over twenty-five years. She was always groomed and dressed in exactly the same way, whatever the occasion: hair pulled back into a bun, white high-necked Victorian blouse, black skirt, and sensible shoes. And never, ever, any makeup. Her severe face and feisty temperament matched perfectly the nickname she had acquired (some said) back when dinosaurs still roamed the earth.

'Think of it this way,' she added. 'Having an ambassador will give you more free time for things you enjoy.'

Godfrey had certainly built a reputation as a Casanova. He gained particular notoriety in his early years by having to be whisked out of Turkmenistan under cover of darkness. Something kinky involving the wife of the foreign minister, her sister, and the French Ambassador's stable boy, it was rumoured. Safely back in Ottawa, he had claimed, 'A small misunderstanding. Merely a case of premature evacuation.'

Alas, he thought to himself, *my skirt-chasing days are almost over too. No self-respecting young female is going to be excited now by a pear-shaped geezer with a fringe of gray hair and a big red-veined nose earned by years of diplomatic drinking.*

Godfrey had found refuge in remote Bharalya, home to one of the last absolute monarchies on earth. Now, suddenly, his cozy life was threatened with work.

'You'd better get busy and organize the *Presentation of Credentials* ceremony,' the Dragon snapped, interrupting his thoughts. 'Those things may be boring but they're important in the diplomatic world.'

'Well, I think they're an utter waste of time! It just means dressing up in fancy clothes, handing over a letter from our government to the King, making a series of vacuous speeches pledging eternal friendship between the governments and people of the two great sovereign nations of Canada and Bharalya, and drinking toasts in tepid Scotch to the longevity of our respective monarchs. Lots of work for nothing. Why not just send each other e-mails and be done with it?'

᎒᎒᎒᎒

Within hours, he was in his air-conditioned limousine on his way to the palace for a meeting with the chief of protocol.

The capital of Bharalya was a half-urban, half-rural place where animals of all kinds—slow-moving water buffalo drooling streams of saliva, sheep tethered for slaughter, goats calmly chewing scraps of garbage, emaciated cattle with flies buzzing on ugly sores, underfed snorting pigs, and ferocious street dogs——all jockeyed with humans and machines for survival.

'What the hell?' he cried in fright to the driver as the gleaming black Mercedes-Benz suddenly lurched to a stop just before making hamburger of a herd of cattle shambling slowly down the dusty road. When the car finally was able to move again, he surveyed the streets through its tinted windows.

Two and three story buildings made from the same reddish-brown brick filled the flat, torrid landscape, adorned only with the occasional coconut palm or tuft of bougainvillea. Tiny houses fashioned from mud, discarded cardboard or metal were clustered up against the more permanent buildings in the vain hope of avoiding being washed away by the next monsoon. Many streets were little more than open sewers; the rancid stench was overpowering in the tropical heat. That Bharalya was among the poorest countries in the world was evident from the rags on the people and the pitiful condition of the fly-blown, runny-nosed children who lined the narrow streets, begging for money or sweets.

There was no plan for the streets; they all ran higgledy-piggledy into narrow alleys. Except, that is, the three main thoroughfares, all of which led directly to the palace. The King had clearly learned something from Napoleon, Godfrey reflected. A clear road where soldiers can move quickly is essential for any self-respecting despot.

The car slowly wound its way to the top of the highest hill overlooking the capital and passed inside a pair of golden gates protecting the palace from the squalor below.

The driver then repeated the same question he asked his passenger every time he passed through the gates, 'Is it not beautiful, sir?'

Godfrey mumbled an indistinct 'harrumph' as he contemplated yet again the garish monument to bad taste and extravagance in front of him. The grandfather of the current King, His Majesty Sasha II, Beloved of His People, Slayer of the Elephant, and Divine Leader of the Kingdom of Bharalya, had constructed it when the British were still in India. It was somewhat smaller than the Vatican but larger than the three hundred and forty-seven-room behemoth constructed by the Maharaja of Jodhpur in India. The King's grandfather had clearly intended to beat the maharaja at his own game. 'Palace envy,' he commented under his breath.

Its style, he thought, would best be described as British imperial monument mixed with South Asian temple, with a dash of rococo thrown in for spice. The entire exterior was covered in white marble. It was so dazzlingly bright in the intense Bharali sunshine, it might have been designed to blind an invader. Huge pillars in the shape of elephants and leopards painted in brilliant reds, oranges, and blues supported golden latticework balconies. Capping the roofline was a series of gigantic golden domes reminiscent of the onion domes on Russian cathedrals, each bearing the insignia of the royal family. And throughout the lush gardens surrounding the place, seven-metre-high statues of His Majesty in his various roles of military commander, chief justice, and spiritual leader were placed ostentatiously.

Godfrey was guided through a magnificent vestibule to a small office just off the main corridor. Along the way, he was again struck not only by the gargantuan proportions of the palace but by the size and number of portraits of the monarch. *It's like a royal fun-house where the King can see his image everywhere he goes,* he thought.

The chief of protocol kept him waiting a further fifteen minutes, as he did all diplomats, to emphasize his rank and importance. Eventually, he swished into the room in his formal white robe and the conical purple cap that indicated he was of royal blood too.

After the obligatory cup of tepid tea, he got down to business. 'As you may know,' he began, 'His Majesty is a collector of foreign honours. In exchange for your ambassador's nomination being accepted by our government, this year His Majesty expects Canada to award him your highest medal and put him on your Honours List. The ceremony will take place two weeks from today. Your ambassador is required to wear your national dress with full decorations.'

CSCSCSCS

Poor Godfrey looked discouraged on his return to the embassy. He fumed all the way up the main staircase to the Dragon's office. 'Medals? Honours?' he shouted. 'How do they expect me to get him the Order of Canada in the next two weeks? I'll need help from Ottawa on this one.'

'Is that all?' she replied scornfully. 'Oh, pooh, don't bother Ottawa with a little problem like that. Some third assistant desk officer in protocol division will only answer you back with a helpful statement such as: "It is the policy of the Government of Canada neither to offer, nor accept, foreign honours." Forget it. Desperate times call for desperate measures. You just relax and work on His Excellency's speech. Leave everything else to me.'

The next day saw a flurry of activity in the embassy. Special parchment paper was borrowed from the Italian ambassador. Hours were spent researching heraldry on the Internet. Supplies from the Dragon's sewing basket were spirited up to the third floor. A set of coins freshly arrived from the mint as promotional gifts was commandeered, as was a box of lapel pins left over from a visit by the mayor of St. John's.

By the end of the day, calm had returned. The embassy's lone colour printer had made the ultimate sacrifice for its country but Godfrey looked like the proverbial cat after dinner with the canary. Even the Dragon was sporting what, for her, might be considered a smile.

C3 C3 C3 C3

Ten days later, His Excellency Percival James Williamson and Madam Marilyn Williamson began the long walk up the red carpet and through the vast foyer of the palace to the Royal Reception Hall.

At the end of the immense mirrored ballroom sat His Majesty, in all his four-feet-nine-inch glory, on a silver throne. To Percy, he looked about forty-five years old but it was hard to be sure at a distance. His head seemed disproportionately large in relation to his tiny body. He sported a graying Salvador Dali mustache which shot out from under his nose at 90 degrees and then curled up into alarmingly sharp points. On his head was the traditional royal Bharali cap of purple silk. His legs were clothed in what appeared to be the local equivalent of capri pants; these made the royal legs look even shorter. On his tiny feet were golden Persian slippers pointed up at the ends, as if imitating the royal face hair.

But what drew gasps from Percy and Marilyn was his coat. The long pastel-blue silk tunic was a sea of medals. They twinkled in the light of the crystal chandeliers like demoniacal Christmas tree decorations. The coat was apparently so heavy that he needed three servants to take it off before he could get up from the throne.

Is that all there is to him? mused Marilyn. *I'll just bet he usually wears platform shoes.*

Percy, however, was watching the almond-shaped eyes, trying to take the measure of the man. The slightly hooded eyelids opened from time to time to reveal a wily, fox-like intelligence. *This is a man to be taken more seriously than he looks,* thought Percy. *One doesn't hold on to absolute power for twenty-five years by being an absolute fool.*

Marilyn, meanwhile, was watching the King's wife, a beautiful, slender woman seated on a lower throne to his right. Her eyes, it seemed, momentarily betrayed her true feelings about His Majesty's addiction to medals, but she quickly reverted to the blank smile required on such occasions. Even queens were expected to know their place in this country.

Percy was dutifully attired in traditional Canadian national dress (at least, that was Godfrey's story for the chief of protocol)—a swallowtail coat decorated with a glittering set of Canadian nickel, dime, and quarter coins attached by ribbons cut from the Dragon's favourite Hermès silk scarf.

Marilyn was also in full regalia, crowned with headgear of operatic dimensions, as recommended by the Foreign Affairs protocol officer before she left Canada. Calling it a hat would be like calling a lion a housecat. It was enormous. What made it really spectacular were the feathers that waved in all directions with every move of her head. There were feathers from Canadian owls, ducks, and geese, and wafting high in the air, a single eagle feather, presumably representing Canada's aboriginal heritage. 'The things I do for my country!' she muttered.

The rest of the Canadians—Godfrey; the Dragon; Sylvie Rajaratnam-Lafrenière, the trade commissioner; Pierre Charlebois, the representative of Canada's international development agency; and Frank Kobayashi, the embassy administrative officer—were decked out like

Royal Doulton figurines. Their role was evidently to be seen but not heard, silent witnesses to a great Canadian historical event.

Pierre even abandoned his principled opposition to suits and ties for the occasion, although he did insist on wearing his perennial sandals to show, as he put it, 'solidarity with the people of Bharalya.'

On a signal from the chief of protocol, Percy and Marilyn glided silently over the ornate Persian carpet to the throne. Percy handed His Majesty a beautiful parchment tied in a red ribbon, and a silver jewel box. Nestled in the box were two decorations, each mounted on a ribbon: a freshly minted one dollar Canadian coin and a lapel pin with the crossed flags of Newfoundland and Labrador.

In a confident voice, he spoke to the King the immortal lines penned by Godfrey:

Your Majesty, in recognition of the high esteem in which Her Majesty Queen Elizabeth II and the Government and people of Canada hold your Royal Highness, and to mark a new era of friendship and cooperation between our two great nations, I am authorized to confer upon you the highest honours offered by my country. By the powers vested in me, I hereby name you Companion of the Loonie and Knight of the Order of St. John's.

The King beamed with pleasure. The Queen arched an eyebrow. Percy smiled his best official smile.

The Dragon whispered into Godfrey's ear: 'You see, there's always a way. If the man wants a blue suit, just turn on a blue light!'

Diplomacy in the Land of Nothing-to-Do

As his limousine drove up to the embassy gates, Percy saw a white stucco colonial-style building set on several acres of manicured green lawn. In the distance, a shimmering blue swimming pool and a red clay tennis court peeked out through feathery palm trees. Were it not for the Canadian flag hanging limply in the breezeless summer air, it could be a golf and country club, he thought. It was a world apart from the poverty just outside.

A guard opened the door of his limousine and saluted as he stepped into the white marble-tiled embassy foyer. He walked up the main staircase to his spacious office past portraits of the Queen and his predecessor ambassadors.

He heard the faint whoosh of air as he settled into a comfortable leather executive chair behind an imposing cherry wood desk. Its pristine surface glowed warmly in the morning sunlight, untainted by papers or electronic devices save two telephones: one black, for everyday use, and one red, a high security phone linking the ambassador with the Operations Room in Ottawa. To the best of anyone's knowledge, the phone had never rung in the twenty years since the embassy was opened. It sat there in serene silence like Keats' Greek urn.

Godfrey was perched on one of the leather visitors' chairs directly opposite, ready for their first official meeting.

'So, Godfrey, what do you suggest I do here in Bharalya?' he asked at last.

Godfrey had his reply down cold.

'There is so much to do, sir. First, there are your obligatory courtesy calls on every ambassador here. That will take up your first month at least. Bloody nuisance though, memorizing all those unpronounceable names and trying to keep the Albanians straight from the Bulgarians.

'On top of that, you *must* attend the national day receptions of all their countries. That's another month per year.

'Then there are the airport runs. His Majesty loves to travel, especially on someone else's ticket. Every time he leaves the country or returns, the entire diplomatic corps has to rush out to the airport like maniacs in their identical black limousines. The palace never gives us much notice. It's a mix of Keystone Kops and state funeral every time. Ambassadors line up for hours like stuffed owls, waiting their turn to express their prayers for his safe return or their government's profound relief when he does so. A ragtag band and chorus treat you to the national anthem, a dreary dirge apparently inspired by a poem His Majesty learned at school:

> *My name is Sasha II, King of Kings,*
> *Look on my Works, ye Mighty, and despair!*

'It's very moving, ahem. Remember to wear comfortable shoes.'

'Yes, yes. Anything else?'

'Then there's the embassy dinner circuit. No one here actually gets to talk to any Bharalis except at official meetings or at the palace. Maybe it's because almost none of us here speaks Bharali. But all embassies have hospitality budgets that must be spent on entertaining somebody; otherwise they don't get any money the next year. The solution: they entertain *each other*! They trot round to each other's houses every night. It's kind of a non-stop, all-you-can-eat buffet in black tie.'

'Oh dear,' said Percy.

'There is a downside to this dining-room diplomacy, of course. Protocol requires everyone to sit at table in order of precedence. That means every evening you and Marilyn will be seated between the same two ambassadors and their wives. This year, you'll be sandwiched between Boristan and North Ennuia. Regrettably, these ambassadors and their spouses speak incomprehensible English and worse French so the small talk may be heavy going. But you'll think of something, I'm sure.

'Speaking of dinners, the big event of the year is the annual dinner at the palace. Everyone must go: the diplomatic corps, their spouses, Bharali ministers, and senior officials. It's one of the rare occasions when ambassadors can start their reports back home with the words that bring an almost orgasmic pleasure to us diplomats everywhere: "*When I dined at the Palace with His Majesty last evening, I raised with him … and he said to me,*" etc, etc.'

'The king's a wily ruler and knows this full well,' interrupted Percy. 'He probably uses hints of non-invitation very effectively to lever free trips abroad.'

Godfrey made no reply, thinking more of the food at the palace. 'The kitchen there is said to be ground zero of the terrible Bharali amoeba. We all start our antibiotics two days before any dinner. Even then, a number of embassies are usually closed for at least a week after.'

'Yes, yes, I can of course handle all that but shouldn't I actually be *doing* something? Like making representations to the government? Giving Ottawa my insights about politics and the economy? Something important?'

Godfrey, horrified, replied immediately. 'Oh no, sir. That's what you have staff for. It would set a terrible precedent for other ambassadors. Raise the bar too high. No, an ambassador's role is to see the big picture, keep his finger on the pulse. That's why you dine with the great and powerful.'

'Like the Boristan and North Ennuian ambassadors, I suppose?'

'Exactly,' said Godfrey.

'Hmmmm,' said Percy, shaking his head as Godfrey left his office.

Godfrey du Tremblay Sutherland-Jones, Percy reflected. The scion of two noble Montreal families. His father reached the lofty level of foreign policy advisor to Prime Minister Lester B. Pearson. His mother was heiress to the du Tremblay pulp and paper fortune. A pity his work ethic never matched the aspirations of his ancestors.

CЗCЗCЗCЗ

Just as Godfrey had predicted, the following weeks were a blur of activity. Yet Percy could not adjust easily to the emptiness of his new existence. His prior life still made him want to believe fate had put in him in Bharalya to do more than fill a chair at the dinner tables of his fellow ambassadors. The problem was, what?

The answer came one morning in the form of a telephone call from the palace.

'It's the chief of protocol for you,' announced the Dragon. 'He says it's important enough to disturb you from your onerous ambassadorial duties.'

Percy soon found out what his 'higher purpose' was. The king wanted him and Madam to do him the honour of judging this year's Chrysanthemum Show. His Majesty was a lover of chrysanthemums, the chief of protocol indicated, and said that the blooms in the palace gardens this year were especially fine.

How can I refuse, thought Percy? *Floral diplomacy—that's all there is to do.*

From that moment on, his life in Bharalya changed. He began to receive an unusually high number of unscheduled visits from his ambassadorial colleagues. The conversations followed a pattern, he noticed. Each would begin with small talk, followed by congratulations on his nomination by the palace and ending—by sheer coincidence— with a reference to the extraordinarily beautiful blooms in his or her embassy's garden. In some cases, there were even hints of air tickets, villas abroad, and cases of wine.

Excitement ran high; for several weeks, the show overshadowed every other topic of conversation on the dinner party circuit. Throughout the diplomatic enclave, gardeners could be seen hard at work bringing each entry to its peak just in time for the competition.

He also began to hear rumours of dirty tricks—stealing flowers at night or knocking down a row or two of pots in the driveway of another ambassador's home after a boozy dinner. The culprit always seemed to blame alcohol but everyone knew better.

CS CS CS CS

Finally, the long-awaited day arrived. He and Marilyn made a fashionably late entrance at the palace. 'To build the excitement,' he said sardonically as they left the residence.

Chrysanthemums in decorated pots and decorated diplomats filled the courtyard outside the Royal Reception Hall. Every eye watched closely as he and Marilyn examined each entry. Whenever Percy made a note in his small black book, an expectant murmur ran through the crowd.

Dinner was announced with a musical fanfare and a call to table by the chief of protocol. On this occasion, Percy was obliged to sit at the head table with His Majesty. He barely survived the last-minute visits by ambassadors or their spouses to remind him of the merits of his or her particular entry. Coffee was being served when the king finally turned to him and indicated the moment had arrived, adding, 'The blooms in my garden were exceptionally fine this year, don't you think?'

On a signal from the king, the chief of protocol invited Percy to the microphone. He was persuasive on any occasion but that night he surpassed himself. He made sure to charm each and every ambassador before announcing his verdict. He flattered this one, stroked the ego of another, and generally succeeded in defusing the tension in the room with his trademark good humour.

At last, he withdrew the little black book from his pocket and told the crowd, 'It was a difficult decision, since there were so many outstanding entries this year. It is unfortunate not everyone can win a prize, much as that would be deserved.'

He went on in this vein for a few more minutes before he came to the climax. The room hushed.

'The winner of the First Prize is … the Embassy of India; Second Prize goes to … the Embassy of Japan; and Third Prize goes to … the Embassy of France.'

He paused, anticipating applause—or at least a reaction—from his audience.

Silence.

He looked around, puzzled. Something had gone terribly wrong in his moment of triumph. His Majesty scowled. The chief of protocol did an excellent impression of a chameleon, his face turning from pink to red to mauve. The three winners-designate sat stone-faced in their seats, nervously eyeing the king.

It was then that the neophyte diplomats present learned what an experienced ambassador can do. Percy smiled broadly and without missing a beat, addressed the king.

"Your Majesty, you will have noticed I have not yet spoken of the chrysanthemums in the Royal Palace gardens. In the view of the judges, they so surpass all the others that they belong in a category of their own. I am pleased to announce that a new prize has been created this year, the Overall Best-in-Show Prize. On behalf of the entire diplomatic community, I am delighted to award this special honour to His Majesty Sasha II, Beloved of His People, Slayer of the Elephant, and Divine Leader of the Kingdom of Bharalya.'

The room exploded in applause. The King, the Indian, Japanese, and French ambassadors and the chief of protocol all broke out in smiles.

'Good for the Canadian ambassador,' was the talk of the room for the rest of the evening.

The King asked Madam for the honour of the first dance and ambassadorial colleagues congratulated Percy on so elegantly resolving what could have become an unhappy incident. Diplomatic harmony was restored.

'*Godfrey was right,*' Percy reflected as he sipped his coffee. '*Ambassadors here only deal with the big issues.*'

Roll Over, Beethoven

Whatever am I going to do in this country? Marilyn pondered. She was seated in her elegant private dining room awaiting the arrival of Henrietta Huntington-Blackstone, the wife of the British ambassador. She was dressed in a simple but elegant blue summer dress set off by a single strand of silver pearls. Her perfect posture and blond hair coiffed in a French twist suggested she might be an art curator or a ballet dancer.

At that moment Henrietta arrived, a portly woman of a certain age wearing a large floral dress and, unnecessary indoors, a large yellow-feathered hat crowned with an imitation bluebird which bobbed with every gesture.

Where on earth does she think she is? wondered Marilyn. *The enclosure at the Royal Ascot?*

After a few minutes of social chit-chat, Marilyn raised the question most on her mind.

'Until now, Henrietta, I was able to carry on my cello career during our postings to Vienna, Beijing, Tokyo, and London. What is there for me to do in Bharalya?'

'Oh, that's easy,' Henrietta tittered gaily, jerking the bluebird into life. 'You just need to join the Diplomatic Wives Association. There are so many wonderful activities, you'll never feel bored. There's bridge, of course. I hope you play. Flower arranging—the Japanese Embassy puts on courses in *ikebana* every year. Badminton, shuffleboard, tennis, synchronized swimming, first aid, language lessons, table etiquette, everything you could possibly want to do.'

'Indeed?' replied Marilyn unenthusiastically. She needed all her self-control to avoid saying something definitely not in the diplomatic lexicon. She was anything but a traditional 'wife of the ambassador'.

Degrees in music at McGill and studies at the Juilliard School had led to a happy marriage with Percy, to be sure, but also to a successful professional life of her own as a musician and writer.

'Bridge, chrysanthemum shows, managing servants, and diplomatic receptions are hardly a life,' she protested.

But Henrietta prattled on, oblivious to her protest. 'Charity bazaars, bingo, visits to orphanages, shopping, more shopping [laugh], the hairdresser's, cooking classes, ballroom dancing, yoga, gardening, music, you name it. Of course, there are some oddballs who try to go it alone. They usually end up fleeing back home or losing themselves in the gin bottle. Let me tell you about one case who...'

'Did you say "music"?' Marilyn said, her interest suddenly piqued. 'You mean Bharali music, I presume?'

Her colleague looked shocked. 'Oh no, *nooobody* here does Bharali music, you know. It's much too foreign for us. I mean the Diplomatic Wives Association Orchestra. Come next week and sit in. They're practicing Beethoven's Ninth for the fall concert.'

'I'm sorry you feel that way about Bharali music. Still, I will come. Music is music, after all.'

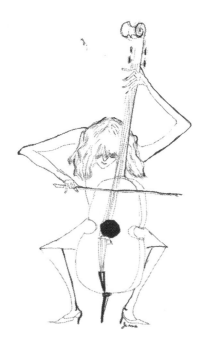

A few days later, she presented herself at the front gate of the German Embassy with her cello in tow. In the distance, she heard sounds of what she at first thought were workshop tools: whining buzz saws, screeching drills, and pounding hammers. *Strange,* she thought, *I must be in the wrong place.* But no, the Bharali guard directed her to the very building that was the source of the earsplitting sounds.

'Excuse me, but is that really where the orchestra practices? Is the building under renovation?'

'Oh, yes, Madam, that is the clubhouse,' he said with a slight roll of the eyes. 'But no, it's not under renovation. That's your orchestra. It sounds a bit, er, unusual to me. But then I'm no expert on your Western music. Good luck, Madam.'

Marilyn passed through the gate, entered the embassy compound, and walked slowly toward the clubhouse. With each step, her apprehension mounted in proportion to the decibel level assaulting her ears. *What have I gotten myself into?* she wondered.

When she opened the door, she was greeted with the most eclectic collection of musical instruments ever assembled for a Beethoven performance. Each wife had brought whatever instrument she played before coming to Bharalya, so the make-up of the orchestra was entirely random and without any connection to the musical score.

She took rapid stock: four flutes, two recorders, a clarinet, a trombone, two French horns, assorted strings, a drum, cymbals, two triangles, a piano, a harp, an accordion, and, amazingly, bagpipes. A Frankenstein orchestra, stitched together from available body parts. *Amazing there aren't steel drums and a hurdy-gurdy too,* she thought.

The players were no less eclectic; the orchestra was a veritable United Nations. The Western Europeans dominated the string section, the Americans had a lock on the harp and piano, the Latin Americans owned the woodwinds, the Eastern Europeans and the Russians had cornered the percussion, and a solitary Scots-Canadian from Cape Breton was czar of the dreaded bagpipes.

Just as she opened her cello case and joined the strings, the conductor, Brunhilde Wagner, spouse of the German Ambassador, raised the baton. She had a commanding presence: six feet tall, blonde hair, two axe-handles in girth. *Likely a direct descendant from the Valkyries,* Marilyn thought. *Well, good. This orchestra needs a strong hand.*

'Ladies, from the beginning again, please.'

Suddenly, the monster honked, squeaked, and rattled to life. Marilyn's ears were attacked by a sound never heard in the halls of Julliard—certainly a sound never imagined by the composer. Frankenmusik! A mash up of traffic noises, animals being tortured, fingernails on blackboards, and faint hints of Beethoven. Her first thought was that if the composer were alive to hear this, he would tear up the score to prevent any further atrocities being visited on the work.

As the orchestra lurched toward the end of the first movement, different sections finished in stages. The triangles finished first, followed soon after by the strings and piano. The accordion and bagpipe straggled over the finish line last, but at least together; their final note was a cacophonous blend of a dying sheep and an unexpectedly unplugged vacuum cleaner.

Oh dear, thought Marilyn.

'Very good, very good,' clucked the conductor, trying to regain through flattery what she had lost in discipline. 'Ten minute break, please, everyone.'

C3 C3 C3 C3

The pause provided Marilyn a chance to meet her bagpiping countrywoman. This turned out to be Megan McAngus, a Cape Bretoner married to a Norwegian diplomat, a jolly woman with a wicked sense of humour.

'Isn't the orchestra just marvellous?' she deadpanned. 'I'm terrible but they're worse! My husband threatens divorce if I ever pipe again at home. The one exception is Robbie Burns Day when I'm allowed to pipe in the haggis. Only then do I crank up the bagpipes and let 'em rip for old Robbie.'

'Norwegians eat haggis?'

'Aye, yes, though I do have to play with the recipe a wee bit. The secret is in the Aquavit. First, I sprinkle the haggis with lots of the stuff and let it marinate for a few hours. While it's brewing, I fill up the guests with enough Aquavit to stun a moose and let them marinate too. They don't remember anything the next day so I tell them they loved it.'

'Where did you learn to read music?' asked Marilyn dubiously.

'Oh, I can't. That's the wonderful part of this orchestra. They're so loud, nobody notices. Whatever the score says, I play tunes I know. The orchestra covers the sound of the bagpipes and I get my practice time in. Everyone's happy. Especially my husband.'

Just then, they were interrupted by the conductor calling them back to their seats. The choir, which had so far been watching from the sidelines, formed up behind the orchestra, ready to sing.

'Now, ladies, we try the last movement, the "Ode to Joy". All together now—one, two, three.'

To Marilyn's mind, the next sign of trouble was that the choir dispensed with the traditional tuning of their voices to the piano. *Likely because they couldn't hold to pitch anyway,* she assumed. And when they began to sing, her worst fears were confirmed.

The sopranos were not just bad; they were crystal-shattering, ear-damagingly bad. *Dangerous in a confined space,* she thought, fearing for the clubhouse windows. The resulting 'Ode' was about as far from joy as it is possible to get. A succession of words reflecting her feelings at that moment ran through her mind: *agony, anguish, distress, torture, martyrdom.* The soaring anthem, which had come to symbolize the European Union, was utterly assassinated by this motley crew.

Mercifully, Brunhilde threw in the towel when several women simply stopped playing in mid-score, announcing they had to leave to prepare dinner parties. Marilyn was delighted to make her escape too, determined never to return.

C3 CB CB CB

A couple of months later, she and Percy were having breakfast when he announced casually, 'I apologize but I forgot to tell you sooner. I've committed us to a concert this evening and dinner after.'

'A concert?' Marilyn perked up, immediately hopeful that one of the embassies was bringing in a famous musician under a cultural promotion program. Or even better, a concert of traditional Bharali classical music. She had recently joined the Bharali women's music group in which the Queen herself played. They had become close friends after discovering a common interest in bringing together the music of Asia and the West. They both admired Yo-Yo Ma's Silk Road project.

'Who's playing?'

'I haven't the faintest, my dear,' he answered absent-mindedly. 'I think it's some orchestra from Berlin. I'm sure you'll love it. And I managed to get us front row tickets.'

C

ଔଔଔଔ

'I've never been in the Bharali National Theatre before,' Marilyn said as they made their way across the foyer and into the main hall. 'Now I know why. It's definitely not the Metropolitan Opera house.'

Years of neglect plus the constant humidity had caused much of the paint to peel from the walls in long strands like giant banana skins. The ceiling was now completely bare of ornament, except for an ancient crystal chandelier dangling precariously from a hook in the middle of what must have once been a rococo painting of cherubs and angels with trumpets. The floor was sticky with generations of spilled food and other substances; she did not want even to speculate what they were. Their shoes squelched as they made their way carefully down the aisle.

'Good evening, Ambassador, Madam,' she heard Percy say over and over as they descended the steps to their seats. 'So wonderful to see you again.' *We of course see these same people every night at some event or other,* she thought cynically. *But that's embassy life here.*

As they reached the front row, she glanced back at the audience packed into the small auditorium.

'The whole diplomatic corps is here,' she whispered to Percy. 'And every male present is dressed identically, in tuxedo and bow tie; the place looks like a colony of stuffed penguins!'

The stage curtain consisted of two sad and tattered pieces of velvet, probably dating back to the 1930s. Perhaps they once had been red—she wasn't sure—but now they were faded to blotches of pink and white, like a tie-dye left too long in the washer. Other than this, the only decoration on the walls was a series of gigantic wooden sculptures of His Majesty celebrating his (non-existent) prowess as a musician. *A nice Stalinesque touch,* she thought.

Suddenly, from behind the curtain, a familiar cacophonic sound like a building being demolished by jackhammers and power saws burst into the hall. In a split second of horrible recognition, Marilyn realized which orchestra was really to play this evening: the Beethoven-massacring Diplomatic Wives' Orchestra. *Tuning up,* she wondered? *Why do they bother? It won't make the slightest difference.*

'I just know you will enjoy this evening,' Percy whispered in her ear at that moment. 'We haven't been to a good concert in so long.' Marilyn winced. The poor innocent had no idea.

The curtain parted slightly and a somewhat embarrassed Wilhelm Wagner, the German ambassador, shuffled out on stage.

'Good evening, ladies and gentlemen,' he shouted, trying manfully to be heard over the horrible noise behind the curtain. 'Welcome to the annual German Embassy classical concert. I am so glad so many members of the diplomatic corps have been able to turn out this evening. I hope you will understand when I tell you I have bad news and good news about tonight's program.

'First, the bad. I regret to inform you that early this afternoon, the Lufthansa airlines flight carrying the Berlin Staatskapelle Orchestra was grounded in New Delhi due to bad weather. I know you will be disappointed, as I am. We seldom have the chance to hear musicians of their calibre here in Bharalya.

'But I do have wonderful news too. The Diplomatic Wives' Orchestra, under the direction of my lovely spouse Brunhilde, has generously offered to advance their Christmas concert and play it for us this evening. As you know, they have been practicing hard these past few months and are now at the peak of their abilities.'

'Meagre,' Marilyn whispered to Percy.

'So, without further delay, please welcome ... our own ... Diplomatic Wives' Orchestra and their unique interpretation of Beethoven's Ninth Symphony.'

Muted applause and much mumbling greeted this announcement. Marilyn noticed several ambassadors who had presumably suffered through this orchestra before quietly slip to the exits. Alas, Percy had committed her to stay the course so escape was out of the question. 'I only wish I had brought those little rubber earplugs the airlines gave me in business class,' she said to him quietly.

The curtain parted. Brunhilde raised her baton and gave the downbeat.

PA-PA-PA-POM! PA-PA-PA-SQWAAAK! responded the orchestra.

'Oh dear,' said Percy.

Soon after it launched into the first movement, the orchestra began to pick up momentum. Unfortunately, in doing so, it sacrificed all common rhythm or pitch. It was not long before it escaped from the conductor's control altogether. Soon it had become like a double-decker bus filled with honking clowns racing the wrong way along a superhighway, a menace to everyone and everything in its path.

The woodwinds and the brass went their separate ways in different keys. The Russian percussionist careened along as if playing a solo; she crashed her cymbals whenever the spirit moved her, irrespective of what Beethoven expected. The Finnish trombonist did a wonderful imitation of a lovesick reindeer mating call. And the bagpiper intervened at random with an ear-destroying combination of squawks, squeals, and cries of pain; in her hands, the instrument proved its origins as a device for spreading fear and trembling among the enemy.

Marilyn surveyed the audience. Smiles were frozen on people's faces and many heads were shaking. Everyone present, including Herr Wagner, had the same thought: 'How soon can I escape?' Alas, there was no intermission. The audience gritted its collective teeth as the concert plunged on towards inevitable disaster.

Suddenly fate intervened in the person of His Majesty Sasha II. Or at least his image. Whether it was the extraordinary vibrations produced by the orchestra or the large number of people crowded into a venue unused for months, nobody could tell. But suddenly, the huge wooden sculptures of the king began to shift from their mountings. One by one, they slid down the walls and crashed onto the wooden floor, then fell over like giant dominoes. Each one produced a resounding BOOM like a cannon shot.

Panic ensued. Those seated near the outer aisles dropped any pretence of diplomatic courtesy and clamoured over one another to get out of the way. Elegantly dressed women tore their dresses and lost shoes as they wrestled with one another in a mad dash for the centre aisle. Tuxedoed diplomats pushed and shoved like teenagers at a rock concert. Soon the entire audience was a seething mass of angry patrons of the arts, pulling hair, scratching, and stomping. It looked like a riot at a World Wrestling Federation match.

The only saving grace was that the orchestra finally stopped playing. 'I'll never forget the image of Brunhilde Wagner at that moment,' said Marilyn later. 'She looked like she had been hit with lightning: jaw dropped open, baton frozen high in the air, eyes out like organ-stops.'

The concert was definitely over.

CXCXCXCX

It was with great relief that Marilyn and Percy eventually made their way to the exit. Standing outside the front door of the theatre while awaiting their car to collect them, she joked, 'Pity they weren't playing the Tchaikovsky 1812 Overture tonight. Those booms would have made a perfect ending for it.'

When their driver finally escaped from the chaotic traffic jam in the parking lot, they settled into the back seat and breathed a sigh of relief.

'At least we have a quiet dinner to look forward to,' said Marilyn. 'By the way, which embassy is it tonight?'

'The Norwegian ambassador's,' Percy replied. 'I accepted when he told me the wife of his Political Counselor is a Canadian and a musician just like you.'

Marilyn stared at him in disbelief.

'And here's the best part. The ambassador has persuaded her to play the bagpipes for us after dinner. I'm sure you'll love it.'

Sex and Politics

As the snow began to fly in Ottawa, the Minister of Natural Resources thought this might be a perfect chance to get away to warmer climes. *I'm tired,* he thought. *It's been a brutal few months of federal-provincial negotiations. An international trip is just what I need. A low-key visit with a little R & R on the side. But nothing too public.*

Bharalya fits the bill perfectly. The country is out of the media spotlight and I can justify the trip as helping the oil drilling negotiations underway. Anyway, time is running out. George Crowley mentioned to me at Cabinet the other day he intends to close it down once those contracts are signed and sealed. And get rid of that ambassador once and for all.

෬෬෬෬

'Sex and politics,' Godfrey was saying to Pierre and Sylvie as they waited for Percy to arrive for the weekly management meeting, 'dangerous individually, incendiary together. The faintest whiff of a *political* sex scandal and Canadians start hyperventilating. Add international travel to the mix and they get absolutely hyper. They enjoy every salacious detail of course, but they pretend they don't."

'Calvinists!' laughed Sylvie, shaking her head in disbelief.

Godfrey pretended he had not heard and carried on.

'Remember the two MPs from different parties caught indulging in a little late-night inter-caucus liaison on the floor of the House? Literally! Unfortunately for them, a technician was testing the television cameras at the time and their tryst was broadcast coast to coast on the public affairs network. Its ratings shot up like a rocket but the star performers paid the price: kicked out of their parties for "Unparliamentary Behaviour".

'And then last year there was that seventy-four year old Senator with a passion for old wines and young ladies. He was supposed to be studying European agricultural policy in Brussels on an inter-parliamentary exchange. He was caught touring the Bordeaux vineyards instead with his special assistant, a gorgeous young intern. It seems she had a passion for generous men of a certain vintage. His wife popped over to Brussels to surprise him and when he couldn't be found, she called in Interpol. Caused an "Ethics in Government" feeding frenzy.'

Percy's arrival turned the discussion to more serious matters. 'We're about to get a ministerial visit,' he announced.

'Yes, I saw the e-mail too,' moaned Godfrey, his lack of enthusiasm palpable. 'Here we go again. This time it's Dan Dickerson, the Minister of Natural Resources, out to promote Canadian oil companies.'

'What do we know about him?' Percy asked. 'We'll have to tailor the visit to his likes and dislikes.'

'Quite a lot, actually,' Sylvie answered. 'He's an oilman himself. Started up a successful exploration business in the Northwest Territories before he went into politics. Has buckets of money, even flies his own airplane. People call him "Diamond Dan".'

'Interesting. What about the man personally?'

'He's tall, fit, and very photogenic. A family values, back to religion, ethics in government politician. Has a beautiful wife, a divorce lawyer in Calgary, and six children. He's a lay preacher in some evangelical church. Serves as chair of the local United Way campaign and is on the boards of several charities for poor mothers and children. Upstanding citizen.'

'Isn't he the one who won the last election in a landslide after the incumbent was caught late one night interviewing his riding assistant with his pants around his ankles?' Percy asked.

'Yes,' Godfrey replied. 'That was when he delivered the famous statement which led to his victory: "No one who breaks his marriage vows should be allowed to hold public office. It is a sacred trust which demands the highest standards of morality."'

'A straight arrow for a change,' Sylvie said with evident relief. She remembered the time in Australia when she swore publicly at a minister who put his hand on her bum during a state dinner: '*Tabernac!* If you don't get your hand off me this minute, Minister, you'll be walking funny all the way home to the outback.' Her mixed Irish and Québecois ancestry had given her fiery red hair and an incendiary personality to match.

Just the kind of high profile visit we needed, she thought. *I'll contact a Canadian journalist I know to make sure someone is here to report on it. The minister will be pleased when he learns the press coverage he got was thanks to us.*

೫ ೫ ೫ ೫

She was with Percy and Godfrey at Royal Bharalya Airport when the minister's plane touched down.

'The Bharali Minister of Energy has decided to pull out all the stops,' she whispered to Godfrey. 'See that honour guard and military band? The program I worked out with him is fabulous— helicopter visits to drilling sites, a huge dinner at the best hotel in town with the cream of the Bharali business community, traffic in the capital stopped for the motorcade, the works. You'd think he was the President of the United States!'

She waved at a Canadian reporter standing in the background in the VIP lounge. *Good,* she thought to herself, *he made it.*

Soon she, Percy, and the minister made their way to the ambassador's waiting limousine and were whisked downtown to the hotel in a fast-moving motorcade with sirens wailing and lights flashing. The minister turned to Sylvie and asked, 'Tell me more about the Minister of Energy. I gather he's a real power in this country.'

'Yes, sir,' she replied. 'He's said to be the second richest man after His Majesty. He owns everything: hotels, factories, oil companies, mines, the national airline, and probably half the land in the capital too. He's known as "Minister Ten Percent". No business deal here is done without his approval—and his commission. In fact, even the hotel you're staying in is his.'

When their limousine pulled up in front of the hotel fifteen minutes later, it was evident all the stops had indeed been pulled out. On the outside of the building in six-foot high letters was a banner saying 'WELCOME CANADIAN MINISTER OF NATURAL RESOURCES DAN DICKERSON' and a billboard-sized colour picture of the man himself looking out over the city. *He looks rather like Mao Tse Tung in Tiananmen Square in China,* Sylvie thought. Dozens of beautiful young Bharali women lined the red carpet leading to the lobby, waving little flags bearing his picture.

'Really high profile, eh?' she remarked. 'Are you pleased, Minister?' He remained silent, much to her disappointment. *I wonder what he is thinking right now,* she asked herself.

What he was really thinking was, *There goes my anonymous little holiday. But at least those Bharali girls are easy on the eyes.*

The rest of the morning passed uneventfully: meetings at the Ministry of Energy, a ribbon-cutting, more press interviews, a tour of the city. Everywhere he went, his picture was conspicuously posted on billboards, buildings, and light poles. No one in the capital could possibly be unaware of his presence, Sylvie noted with pleasure.

A sumptuous lunch in the hotel dining room followed. At the end of the meal, she heard the Bharali minister lean over and whisper to her minister in a conspiratorial tone, 'I'm sure you must be tired after your morning's activities. It is the custom in our country to take a rest in the afternoon, to refresh ourselves for the evening. I will leave you now but I look forward to seeing you again at dinner. My staff will take care of you in the meantime.'

With that, an aide escorted them back to the lobby. To Sylvie's surprise, he did not stop at the elevators to the rooms but continued on to a door on the opposite side. They crossed a small alley and entered another building. Godfrey suddenly realized where they were headed. He tried his best to stop the aide, but Percy (who did not understand) told him not to make such a fuss and to carry on.

A last door opened and they saw a sight beyond their wildest imagination—at least, Sylvie's and Percy's imaginations.

'*Merde!*' she exclaimed.

They were in an enormous room covered in burgundy velvet. Mirrors were everywhere on the walls and the ceiling. A band, fronted by an absolutely gorgeous young singer in a slinky gold sarong, played Western popular music softly. On the circular benches in the centre of the room, a hundred or more temptingly beautiful young women were seated, each wearing a number—and very little else.

'What's going on, Godfrey?' she asked in a worried voice.

'Just go with the flow. The minister is about to meet Bharali hospitality.'

She couldn't believe her ears when a beautiful Bharali hostess glided over to them and embraced the minister warmly, cooing in a sultry voice: 'Welcome to our little club, Mr. Dickerson. We are also honoured to meet you, Mr. Ambassador. This is the first time we have had the pleasure; I hope it will not be the last.' Finally, noticing Godfrey she added, 'So nice to see you again, Godfrey. Where have you been hiding?' Sylvie looked daggers but said nothing as the hostess took his hand and pointed to the young ladies.

'Now, Minister, it is for you, as our honoured guest, to choose first.'

To Sylvie's astonishment, the minister did not hesitate for a second. Turning to Sylvie, he said with a wink, 'Other countries, other customs, eh? What happens in Bharalya, stays in Bharalya, right?' Before she could say a word, he rushed off with the hostess to see the young ladies. She overheard only a few words of their conversation but was almost certain he asked if he could have two.

She was outraged. All her instincts were to tell the Bharalis in words of one syllable what they could do with their 'hospitality' and frog-march the minister out the nearest door. Her temper was on the point of exploding and her face showed it. Percy sprung into action just in time. The last thing he needed was a diplomatic incident *and* an angry minister.

'Sylvie, let's get out of here. Godfrey, you stay and keep an eye out for the minister. Make sure he gets back to the hotel.' Godfrey's face showed that this was an assignment he was delighted to handle.

Percy had visions of the minister's career in ruins if the press got wind of his foray into Bharali 'hospitality'. But the situation was now out of his hands. 'At least there was no Canadian press covering the visit,' he said as they crossed the alley.

Sylvie made no reply. She had already decided not to inform him of such a minor detail as the presence in the massage parlour of the Canadian journalist she had contacted. *'Que sera, sera,'* she was humming as they re-entered the lobby.

CR CR CR CR

As the minister settled into his seat on the plane for Canada at the end of his program, he reflected on the pleasures of the visit, secure in the knowledge that his experience of Bharali customs would remain secret. He had in fact always appreciated the discretion of the Foreign Service. He had a long history of enjoying the delights available during his travels abroad and counted on the embassies to cover his tracks.

'We'll just keep this in the family, right, Ambassador?' he said with a conspiratorial wink as they shook hands at the airport. It was an order, not a question.

'A diplomatic secret, Minister,' Percy reassured him.

During the long flight to Europe, Dickerson slept fitfully, thinking of his return to the pressures of Parliament. 'Still, best job I've ever had,' he mused contentedly. 'And the fringe benefits … wonderful!'

Hours later in Frankfurt, he boarded the Air Canada flight to Ottawa for the last leg of his journey. Seated comfortably in business class and enjoying a glass of complementary champagne, he decided to glance at the Canadian newspapers on offer by the hostess. His life flashed before his eyes as he read the headline in the *Toronto Star:*

MINISTER CAUGHT IN BHARALYA BROTHEL
RESIGNATION DEMANDED

When the story broke, the inevitable panicked e-mails from Foreign Affairs' headquarters and the Prime Minister's Office were flashed to the embassy. Percy had to confirm that the story was true but was able to reply with complete honesty that he had no idea a Canadian journalist was in town.

Sylvie was uncharacteristically tight-lipped on that score. However, she was heard to comment when the minister's resignation was announced, '*Merde*, you live by the sword, you die by the sword.'

The Year of the Tourist

'Ambassador,' said the Dragon, 'I think there is something you should know about Pierre and Godfrey.'

'You mean they're an item?' asked Percy, straight-faced. It amused him to wind her up and it always worked. The Dragon, whose sense of humour was said to have been surgically removed in childhood, glared at him icily.

'No, no. Just the opposite,' she insisted. 'It's practical jokes. They've been going on since Godfrey arrived. Pierre can't seem to stop.'

'Godfrey's probably a target because he was born with the proverbial silver spoon. Since he was admitted to Foreign Affairs, it has never occurred to him he is expected to actually do anything beyond gracing us with his presence.'

'That's maybe part of it, sir. Pierre comes from a working class family. He earned his way through university the hard way. But mainly, I think it's because Godfrey refuses to get out of the diplomatic enclave and see the real country. Pierre knows more about this country than the rest of the embassy put together. He speaks wonderful Bharali.'

'Anyway, tell me, what sort of jokes are we talking about?' Percy knew he would enjoy them too, even if he dared not share his pleasure with his lugubrious assistant.

'Manure, sir.'

'Excuse me?'

'A huge pile of manure, sir. Pierre had a truckload of steaming water buffalo droppings delivered to Godfrey's house just before he was to host a large dinner party on his patio. The guests arrived to an overwhelming *parfum du barnyard* and a three foot-thick cloud of buzzing flies. The evening was a complete fiasco! Godfrey lost face with all the other embassies.'

'Sounds very serious indeed,' said Percy, barely suppressing a smile. Godfrey wouldn't go to the country so the country came to him. 'Any, aah, other "situations"?'

'Oh, yes, sir, there have been many. Pierre once had his interpreter place an advertisement in the *Bharalya Times* announcing Godfrey's forthcoming marriage. It took Godfrey weeks of explaining to his Bharali contacts why they had not been invited to the wedding. And after that there was the poker night. Pierre persuaded Godfrey to come to his poker club but did not tell him what the stakes would be until they started to play.'

'Let me guess who went home with nothing in his wallet.'

'Exactly, sir. Godfrey styles himself an expert player. He thought it would be *he* who taught the poker club a lesson that night. He was very put out.'

'It was lucky they weren't playing strip poker,' Percy almost said but caught himself in time. 'All right, I'll look into it,' he promised. 'Thank you for bringing this important issue to my attention.'

Satisfied she had done her duty, the Dragon lifted her nose in the air, tossed her head, and returned to her lair.

CECECECE

'Godfrey, you have to get out and see the country more,' Pierre was saying. 'Come with us this weekend. There's a riverboat that goes all the way down to the Bay of Bengal. It's a working boat, but they have a few cabins. Adventure of a lifetime.'

'Yes, Godfrey, you really must come,' echoed Sylvie. She had secretly been recruited as Pierre's co-conspirator on this occasion. 'It's *The Year of the Tourist* in Bharalya. Haven't you seen the posters? The riverboat is being advertised as the country's major tourist attraction.'

Pierre knew full well that Godfrey was always skeptical when His Majesty's government proclaimed anything. The current announcement, The Year of the Tourist, was no exception. In this case, he was right. The tourist tsunami trumpeted by His Majesty's Ministry of Tourism had, so far, only amounted to one busload of Dutch tourists and a gaggle of assorted backpackers. Hardly a flood of high-spending visitors.

'Why on earth would I want to go?' Godfrey protested. 'Have you forgotten what it's like out there? Insufferable heat, bugs and dirt. If the climate doesn't get me, the amoeba will. Look at what happened to that group of Canadian tourists last year. Their bus broke down and they found themselves stuck in the middle of nowhere for three days. They ran out of food and water and had to live off the land. Half of them came down with Bharali Bowels. Not a pretty sight when they got back here. They demanded I lodge a protest with the Tourism Minister. Lot of good that would do them, or us. No, thank you very much, I'll take air conditioning and clean sheets every time!'

'Godfrey,' asked Pierre, 'in the four years you have been here, how many times have you actually gone outside the capital?'

'Just once, actually, and that was enough for me. I had to accompany some visiting Pooh-Bah from the Canadian Fertilizer Association. It was the Bharali amoeba that laid me low from the very first day. It lasted almost two weeks. You should have seen the toilets there. Just a hole in the ground, two footpads and a bucket—if you were lucky. Unspeakable! I plan never, *ever* to set foot outside the embassy district again until I go to the airport to leave this country forever.'

'Nonsense, Godfrey. It will make a man of you. Pack your diarrhea medecine, but come. We'll even take a picnic cooler with your own food, if that makes you feel better.'

His facial expression said it did not. Given a choice at that moment, he would have opted for an appendectomy over the indignities of in-country travel. But when Percy finally insisted that he come, he was cornered. For the next few days, he had the look of a condemned man walking to the scaffold.

C3 C3 C3 C3

When they met him at the pier, what was astonishing was not his attitude but his attire. Everyone else was in casual outfits—jeans, safari suits, Tilley hats, and the like—but Godfrey was impeccably dressed in business suit, tie, and brogues polished to mirror sheen. He looked as if he should be in the reception line at an embassy dinner—his preferred location, in fact. He was determined not to be mistaken for a tourist, and he succeeded. But not in the way he expected. He stuck out like the statue of some long-gone colonial official around which a sea of brilliantly-clothed Bharalis and their animals swept to the boat.

The scene was chaotic. Great bales of cargo, water buffalos and pigs were being winched into the hold on coir ropes. Half-naked men, sari-clad women, scruffy children, sheep, goats, dogs and chickens rushed, pushed and pulled their way up the gangplank, all accompanied by a din of yells, cries, bleating, barking and clucking. Vendors calling loudly from shore to the passengers hawked fruit and food. Listless police officers made ineffectual efforts to keep order.

The vessel was designed for three hundred but was already filled well past its capacity. People were everywhere: on the top deck, on the lower decks, even hanging onto the wrong side of the rails. Hundreds more were still streaming forward, threatening to sweep Godfrey away in a human and animal tidal wave.

An official from the Tourism Ministry was on the pier. He knew Godfrey and called out to say hello. Distracted, Godfrey did not watch his step and planted a beautifully shod foot up to the ankle in a steaming pile of water buffalo dung. He was not amused.

'Now he's really put his foot in it,' Pierre cracked.

When they eventually reached their cabins, it was immediately evident to Godfrey that he was not on a luxury liner. 'Spartan' would be a generous description. A metal bedstead manufactured when Queen Victoria still reigned and a small bedside table were the only furniture. The room was lit with one naked bulb hanging from a frayed wire. Seeing the horror on Godfrey's face, Pierre made his move.

'Godfrey,' he said, pointing to the middle cabin, 'you take the largest one. I'll have the food and drinks put in with you, in case you need something during the night.'

CR CR CR CR

Determined not to enjoy a moment of the trip, Godfrey spent the whole day in the bow of the boat, silently scanning the horizon like a goddess on the prow of an ancient warship. Maybe he was praying, the others thought—no doubt for his safe (and instantaneous) return to the diplomatic district.

Bharalya from the river was a different country from Bharalya on the plains or in the mountains. The river teemed with human and animal life. Its banks were crowded with hundreds of villages where the river clearly played a central role in the lives of the inhabitants; everywhere there were people fishing, swimming, bathing, and washing clothes. Country boats glided by, graceful with billowing square sails in hues of blue, green, yellow, and ochre. They conjured up images of Egypt and the *feluccas* on the Nile.

As it descended toward the Bay of Bengal, the river widened out into a vast lake whose shorelines were no longer visible. Shifting sandbars appeared or disappeared overnight. The ever-changing riverscape in front of them was like a wide-screen movie playing for their personal pleasure.

At dusk, dinner was served in the 'dining room', an empty space on deck near the 'first class' cabins. A canvas roof flapped above a few tables set up haphazardly. As they expected, the fare was modest but adequate: rice and grilled fish spiced with Bharali vegetable pickles. Fearing for his intestines, Godfrey refused to join them. He dined instead in his cabin on peanut butter sandwiches and Coca Cola.

They did not hear from him again until they were awakened shortly after midnight by a blood-curdling scream. They rushed to his door, fearing the worst. There they found him sitting rigid on his bed, shivering with fear, feet in the air to escape any contact with the floor. He was screaming like a baby.

By the light of the bulb swinging over his bed, they saw what had reduced their cynical diplomatic colleague to this sorry state. The walls and floor of the cabin were shimmering and pulsating like waves on the river. It took a few seconds for their brains to absorb what their eyes were seeing; the entire cabin was covered in cockroaches, *hundreds* of cockroaches.

Godfrey's in-room dining and the picnic coolers had proven an irresistible attraction to these voracious roaches. While his colleagues had been dining insect-free (thanks to him) just a few feet away, he had unintentionally rung the dinner bell for all the insect passengers on their deck. And every last one had taken up his invitation.

When he calmed down enough to talk, he said he heard crunching and scratching as soon as he turned out the light. As the sounds got louder and louder, he turned the light back on. The Horror! There, in front of his eyes, was his worst nightmare. 'Look,' he shouted, gesturing wildly around the room, '*these* are why I didn't want to come on your infernal voyage. This is the last time I will *ever* travel on this insectarium again!' Then, grabbing his clothes and shoes, he rushed out of the cabin, leaving the others shaking with laughter.

Needless to say, the rest of the voyage was for Godfrey the 'Voyage of the Damned'. He remained sleepless on deck the entire night, dressed in his suit, refusing to set foot in the cabin again. He swore he would neither eat nor drink until they arrived back in the capital.

An official from the Ministry of Tourism was there when they landed in the southern-most river port the next morning. Godfrey leapt from the boat, flashed his diplomatic card, and announced to the startled man: 'I must get back to the capital immediately. Urgent diplomatic business. Very important to His Majesty that I return without delay. The business of state, etc., etc.'

In the face of a potential international incident with a diplomat in full regalia—not a sight often seen in this small town a world away from the capital—the poor official did not at first know what to do. But the mention of the king galvanized him into action, probably for the first and only time in his civil service career. He picked up Godfrey's bags and personally drove 'His Excellency' directly to the local airport.

છ છ છ છ

'*Godfrey du Tremblay Sutherland-Jones, Tourist of the Year?*' read Percy, amazed. He and Pierre were in his office, looking at Godfrey's face staring back at them from the cover of the Ministry of Tourism's glossy promotional magazine, *Visit Beautiful Bharalya*. Godfrey was dressed in the same suit and tie he had worn on the trip a month earlier.

'Unbelievable, isn't it?' chuckled Pierre. 'I guess they don't often get diplomats on that boat. Someone must have told the Minister of Tourism because the minister called him up personally to offer him the title. Godfrey accepted and now he's the official poster boy for the *Bharalya Year of the* Tourist!'

'*Someone?*' asked Percy, looking directly at Pierre with a knowing smile.

Pierre merely shrugged. 'Just wait until he finds out what goes with the honour. The winner is committed to visiting all five regions of the country this year! *Bon voyage, Godfrey!*'

Piggy and the Foreign Minister

'What exactly does Wigglesworth do here at the embassy?' Percy inquired. 'He never seems actually to do anything and he certainly is never at embassy functions.'

'You mean Piggy?' replied the Dragon, rolling her eyes. 'Trouble wherever he goes. A walking time bomb, that one. He used to cut a broad swath through the diplomatic cocktail circuit back in Ottawa. It was absolutely the worst environment for someone whose brain short-circuits at the faintest whiff of alcohol.

'I'll never forget the memorable moment when he mistook the Mexican ambassador's wife for a potted palm, and poured the remains of his whiskey and several hors d'oeuvres into her lap. Or the time when he was well lubricated at a reception at Rideau Hall and fell onto the first soldier of the Governor General's honour guard. Single-footedly, he knocked the whole line of them down like ten-pins and came to rest on top of Her Excellency, nose ensconced in the Vice-Regal bosom.'

'Oh, he's the one?' replied Percy. 'Now I remember. Stories about his performance appraisal also used to circulate around the department. The best gems were recited to shrieks of laughter in the cafeteria:

> *Diplomats are usually born with silver spoons in their mouths; Wigglesworth was born with a foot in his, and nothing suggests that he has changed position since joining the Department.*

> *Wigglesworth continues to slide down the career ladder; this year he appears to be gaining momentum.*

Wigglesworth is like a losing racehorse: comes out of the starting gate well but unfortunately facing the wrong way. The humane thing might be to shoot.

I seem to recall the director of personnel also placed a personal notation on his confidential file:

Posting to Bharalya to be renewed indefinitely until Wigglesworth expires or retires, whichever comes first. Preferably the former.

'That's your man, sir. So when Godfrey became *chargé d'affaires* here, he took immediate steps to protect what remained of his career from the sort of damage of which Piggy was uniquely capable. Piggy was confined to barracks. Since then, he has spent all day clipping newspapers. He is only let loose to go to the airport to help Canadian visitors—of whom there are mercifully few—through customs and immigration.

'As far as I know,' she continued, 'everything was fine until the foreign minister made an unplanned visit here last year. That's when fate, in the person of Piggy, brought Godfrey's career crashing down yet again.'

'Really? It wouldn't take much to do that.'

'The foreign minister was on an important visit to Beijing and New Delhi, accompanied by a dozen journalists and a gang of aides and Foreign Affairs mucky-mucks. At the last minute, he decided to include a short stop-over in Bharalya. The minister saw it as "an opportunity to promote Canadian oil and gas interests", or so his office told a skeptical embassy.

'We had only two days notice. Everyone had to pitch in. And that meant letting Piggy off his leash. Godfrey decided the safest course was to keep Piggy as far away from the embassy as possible. That's when he made his Big Mistake. He came up with the idea of sending him to Beijing to fly in with the ministerial entourage. That way, he thought, logistical arrangements could be ironed out with the minister's staff right on the plane.'

'Oh-oh,' clucked Percy.

'Your intuition is right, Ambassador. What Godfrey could not foresee was that a monsoon storm would roar up from the Bay of Bengal and intersect the minister's route just as he entered Bharali territory. The plane was diverted to wait out the storm at the only other airport in the country, in the western region where the king's brother is governor.

'The foreign minister was happy to have a little extra time to study the briefing book for his Indian visit and gave orders not to be disturbed. His wishes were enforced to the letter by his chief of staff, affectionately known to journalists and aides by the name of "She Who Must Be Obeyed". Silence reigned. Hip flasks kept the press corps happily tranquilized. The mucky-mucks plotted strategy in hushed tones. Junior aides frowned and looked at their watches, worried by this—as by any—change from the script.

'As the plane taxied to a stop, an ancient Russian Lada and a rusty bus drove out to meet it. A once-red carpet was rolled to the foot of the steps leading to the plane. From the limousine and bus emerged the governor in full dress uniform, accompanied by a photographer and a bedraggled ten-piece military band. The governor insisted he must have a *personal word* with the minister before he could authorize the plane to continue its unscheduled flight to the capital.

'Conscious of the minister's orders, "She Who Must Be Obeyed" looked around desperately for someone, anyone, wearing a suit and tie. That someone turned out to be our boy Piggy. Innocent of his potential for mayhem, she summoned him to the front of the plane and ordered, "Go out there, pretend you're the minister, and get us out of here as fast as possible."

'I'm told Piggy drew himself up to what he hoped would pass for ministerial height and descended the steps, flashing a salute to the military band and a broad, if slightly drooling, smile to the governor.

'Now, Piggy had seen *part* of the embassy's briefing for the minister. He knew the king was going to press Canada to increase aid to his country, demand more foreign investment in the energy sector, and ask for an official invitation to visit Canada. Unfortunately, he had not been given access to what the minister was actually to say. In these circumstances, he fell back on the only lesson he remembered from basic training: A*lways maintain good relations with the host country.*

'After shaking hands, he began to speak. Improvising as he went along, he said Canada would be doubling its aid program to Bharalya, and would be sending an oil and gas industry mission within months. Based upon his personal intimate relationship with the Governor General, he was certain she would be thrilled to receive an official visit from His Majesty and even have him stay with her at Rideau Hall.

'The governor's beaming smile and farewell wave brought relief to the chief of staff who could observe—but not hear—this exchange from inside the plane. "Well done, Wigglesworth," she said warmly on his return. "The minister will be very grateful."

෬෬෬෬

'An hour later, the plane landed at Royal Bharalya Airport. The minister and his entourage flooded out, unaware of the disaster about to engulf them.

His Majesty and Godfrey, puffed up like two male peacocks courting the same female, put on their best official smiles as the minister descended from the plane. Godfrey extended his hand, saying, "Welcome to Bharalya, sir." But the king stayed immobile, looking past the minister in the direction of the plane.

'Minutes passed. The minister was speechless.

'Had Godfrey known that the governor had earlier wired his brother a report of Piggy's promises and Piggy's photograph, he would not have been so relaxed and confident when he said, "Nothing serious, Minister. It's only Bharali protocol. Always unpredictable."

'Piggy finally emerged from the plane, the very last person. His Majesty beamed and signalled to the band to play "O Canada" and the Bharali national anthem. He hugged Piggy, kissed him on both cheeks, and the spoke into the waiting microphone. "Welcome to the Kingdom of Bharalya, Minister. Your increase of Canadian aid and investment is most generous and I accept your offer to stay with the Governor General unconditionally."

'And looking Godfrey in the eye, he added, "I am sure your ambassador here will be most pleased to arrange my state visit to your beautiful country without delay."

'Leaving Godfrey and the minister gobsmacked on the tarmac, His Majesty took Piggy by the arm and said, "Now, Minister, we have much to discuss. Please do me the honour of accompanying me to the palace in the royal limousine."'

'So what happened to Godfrey?' Percy asked.

The Dragon answered by handing him two clippings from the *Globe* and *Mail* (presumably clipped by Piggy himself):

CANADA TO EXPAND ECONOMIC RELATIONS WITH KINGDOM OF BHARALYA

ACTING CANADIAN AMBASSADOR TO BHARALYA RECALLED TO OTTAWA

Potemkin Village

'The official visit season seems to be heating up,' said Percy. Looking at the unenthusiastic faces of his colleagues around the boardroom table, he added, 'I know you are looking forward to it as much as always.'

'It's as predictable as the migration of Canada geese,' chimed in Godfrey, pouring himself a cup of tea. 'Official visits and how to avoid them' was one of his favourite subjects.

'The temperature back home drops below freezing, Parliament takes a break, and bang, a "Visit to the Field" suddenly becomes of burning importance,' added Pierre. 'The mucky-mucks in Valhalla think our foreign policy priorities come from those turgid papers they send to ministers. Nonsense! Show me a country where the climate is warm (but not too hot) between November and March and I'll show you next year's new priority country. All it takes is a twenty-four hour ministerial visit.'

'*Tabernac*, that's so true,' echoed Sylvie. 'Consider Iceland or Norway. How many visits do you think they get between November and March? Then look at the Caribbean or even our own little piece of paradise here.'

'Now, now, colleagues,' soothed Percy. 'A ministerial visit is always a Good Thing. It promotes better relations between our two countries and gives the embassy, quite frankly, a *raison d'être*.' *Goodness knows we need one here,* he thought to himself.

What he did not say was that a ministerial visit would also be an excellent excuse for him to ask for meetings with the Minister of Foreign Affairs and the Minister of Finance. As ambassador, he had an agenda of his own to push, never mind a visiting minister's.

Competition for the presence of senior Bharali ministers at embassy Christmas functions was fierce, he knew. *I have been waiting for just this opportunity to urge them to attend our party. I have no intention of losing my standing in the diplomatic corps after my coup at the Chrysanthemum Show, he thought.*

'Well, sir,' announced Pierre, 'here's the next goose of the season. As it were, of course. The Minister for Development Cooperation. We just received a message from her chief of staff. She says the minister wants to come here next month.'

'What does she want to do?' asked Percy.

'Apparently she wants to see (and I quote), "Real Development at the Grassroots Level"—a typical Bharali village, that sort of thing. Wants pictures of herself with villagers doing something faintly industrial (but not too industrial; no labour relations or workplace safety issues, please). She'd also like to lay the cornerstone for a new building so she can take back proof that Canada's aid program is getting concrete results.'

Groans all round.

'Sorry, but I couldn't resist,' chuckled Pierre. 'Anyway, the kicker is she can only spend half a day in this country, so she can't travel too far from the capital.'

'And the usual guff about no errors, I suppose? Heads will roll, that sort of threat?'

'Of course. The chief of staff didn't mention drawing and quartering specifically, but that's always the message.'

Sylvie, ever practical, was doing the math. 'A cup of tea at the foreign ministry requires an hour, and another at the Ministry of Finance will take almost the same,' she said. 'That leaves only three hours for the village project visit and the cornerstone ceremony, including travelling time. That will be a tight schedule.'

Percy turned to Pierre and said pleasantly, 'Well, I'm sure you can put something together to keep the minister happy.'

Pierre, usually boisterous and outgoing, was suddenly quiet. His mind was whirring through the list of Canadian development projects. Canada only had a small aid program in Bharalya—in fact, very small after the latest budget cuts: a project to help the country draft its first human rights legislation; another to teach parliamentary procedure to Bharalya's so far impotent Parliament; and a couple of mini hydroelectric installations way up in the mountains. Alas, no village industries and no buildings to inaugurate.

'We don't have any projects like that,' he finally declared. 'Most of what we do have is located a hundred kilometers away up north or in government ministries here in the capital where there's nothing to see.'

Godfrey suddenly cheered up. 'So it's impossible?' he asked, hoping in his heart he could nip this visit in the bud.

After a period of silence, a small smile flickered across Pierre's face. 'No, Godfrey, not totally impossible. Let me think about it.'

03 03 03 03

As it happened, Percy and he were about to leave for the monthly Aid Coordination luncheon hosted by the United Nations Resident Representative. Every ambassador of a country with an aid program in Bharalya attended, along with the senior aid specialist. Though they all wondered why.

As they drove there in his limousine, Percy wisely observed, 'Everyone there is absolutely in favour of coordination … as long as they are not the ones being coordinated.' The fact is, no one wants to face the sticky reality that it's ultimately the job of the host country to coordinate *them*. As a result, nothing of real importance is ever put on the luncheon agenda. This allows the discussion to flow like the wine on more important topics. Like the horrors of ministerial visits.

Over coffee, Percy outlined his dilemma and asked for advice. There was much sympathetic clucking and stories of official visits past.

'Let me tell you my favorite story,' said the German ambassador. 'I once had a minister who got into a drinking contest during a state dinner at the palace. You all know the local drink here, *rakkal*? No? Well, it's a kind of toddy made from the fermented sap of palm trees. It's as potent as aircraft fuel. The Bharalis love to egg on unwary foreigners to match them glass for glass in toasting mutual health and prosperity. It gives them the upper hand at negotiations the next day. No foreigner ever comes out on top and this time was no exception.

'My minister gradually slipped lower and lower in his chair, rolled off with a grunt, and ended up under the table, face down, snoring like a chain saw. He eventually regained semi-consciousness and made his way to the door on hands and knees while the official speeches droned on overhead. All present, including me, kept their eyes averted, as if nothing happened.'

The American ambassador regaled them with his own tale, the visit of his Secretary of Energy. 'Bharali offices have twelve foot high windows with long flowing curtains to keep out the sun, but no glass. When the wind blows, and it blows hard at some times in the year, those curtains swing wildly. They have been known to sweep cups of tea, biscuits, and flower arrangements into the laps of unwary visiting foreigners.

'My Secretary of Energy was a Texas oil man in his past life, with a highly aggressive approach to negotiations and little time for protocol. His style had begun to grate right away on the Bharali government. Everyone looked forward to seeing him off as soon as possible, and no one more than myself.

'He was famous for dozing off during international meetings, being more susceptible to jet lag than most. An aide was usually at his side to give him a well-directed elbow as required. Unfortunately, on this occasion the seating plan placed his aide out of range.

'The afternoon sun warmed the room and the curtains swirled hypnotically. He soon nodded off. Then a sudden gust of wind sent a curtain towards him and before anyone could move, his head was wrapped in a gauzy cocoon like an Egyptian mummy. Catching my eye, the Bharali Minister gestured to me to do nothing.

'"Best to let sleeping dogs lie," he said with a wink. The meeting carried on to its end, interrupted only by occasional snorts from the mummy. It was only when the meeting ended that I nudged him awake and reassured him the meeting had gone very well.'

'Your problem, Percy,' offered the Danish ambassador, the longest-serving member of the diplomatic corps, 'is one we have all encountered. I have good news for you. We put our heads together a few years ago and found a *coordinated* solution. We call it "The Potemkin Manoeuvre." I recommend you consider it.'

Percy turned to Pierre. Pierre confirmed it was indeed true, though he did wonder whether his new ambassador would have the courage to try such an irreverent move on the minister. He personally was delighted to take the risk but he knew if it failed, it would be the ambassador's head on the chopping block.

'I'll take care of it, but don't ask me any questions, Ambassador. There are some things you are better off not knowing.'

ଔଔଔଔ

A month later, the Canadian Minister for Development Cooperation, her chief of staff, and a photographer emerged from the plane for the five-hour ministerial tour. After a short briefing at the embassy, a motorcade led by Percy's limousine headed out of the city. Pierre offered a running commentary on the country and on life in Bharali villages. Had the minister and her chief of staff not been distracted by this non-stop conversation, they might have noticed that the car had been driving slowly in a circle around the city and was now headed back toward the starting point.

Eventually, they turned into a road lined with Bharali children miraculously waving Canadian flags.

A homemade banner stretched over the entrance to the village, welcoming the minister in best Bharali English. However, the 'Spinister' had no time to react. She was immediately draped in garlands and escorted to a makeshift viewing stand in the centre of the village.

The mayor spoke passionately (through an interpreter) about how the Canadian aid program had brought a big improvement to their lives. Thanks to her country's generosity, he said, the villagers were now earning income. In fact, they had put aside enough money to build the village's first school. He invited the minister, whose visit *by chance* coincided with the laying of the cornerstone, to preside over the ceremony.

The chief of staff, now relaxed, smiled at Pierre. Pierre winked back.

The minister was then treated to traditional Bharali dancing by the girls of the village. The photographer bounced and bobbed in all directions, catching for posterity (and election posters) those beautiful shots of the minister surrounded by happy village women. She was given a conducted tour of the 'factory', a pleasant open-air building where women were weaving, making pottery, and wrapping souvenirs for sale to tourists.

The woman in charge presented the minister with a selection of Bharali handicrafts as a souvenir of her visit 'which we will cherish forever,' she said. Finally, the minister cut the ribbon and laid the cornerstone inscribed with her name (only slightly misspelled), again to the evident joy of her photographer.

It had been a perfect day: bright sun, blue sky, happy villagers, warm embraces, mutual declarations of undying friendship, and excellent photos. Even the politically battle-hardened chief of staff had a small tear in her eye as she and the minister said farewell and returned to the car. Travelling a route vaguely reminiscent of the one taken earlier, they arrived back in the capital for her courtesy calls at the foreign ministry and the Ministry of Finance.

Five hours to the minute from her touch-down at Royal Bharalya Airport, the minister was ready to re-board her plane. Grasping Percy by the hand, she thanked him for a wonderful and memorable visit. The chief of staff congratulated Pierre on his excellent arrangements.

CB CB CB CB

At that very same moment, on a piece of vacant land three blocks from the Canadian Embassy, another scene of congratulations and thanks was under way.

Pierre's cook, various Bharali employees of the German, British, French, and Spanish ambassadors and their friends and families were busy taking down the banner, dismantling the factory, and putting the handicrafts into storage boxes. The Dragon was handing out envelopes of money.

'That went well, as it always does,' said the 'mayor' of the village, in the exquisite English perfected during his years as a student at the London School of Economics. As he continued changing into his regular clothes as the Bharali administrative officer at the Italian Embassy, he added: 'I thought the banner misspelling was a particularly nice touch.'

'We have to rush off now,' Pierre's cook said. 'Tomorrow it's a Swedish parliamentary committee coming to see village health care and we don't have the Swedish flags made yet. Later this week, we're to be a dairy cooperative for a British minister.'

The 'mayor' shook hands good-bye and said to the Dragon with a broad smile, 'This has turned out to be the best income-generating aid project in the whole country. Please tell Pierre to call on us again any time. We appreciate your business.'

Swimming with Diplomats

'There must be a foreign policy crisis or else news about closing the embassy,' the Dragon said to Percy and Godfrey. 'Your management committee ran for three hours yesterday.'

'No, no, it was something *much* more serious,' Godfrey explained. 'Diarrhea.'

Her mind boggled. She remembered a Canadian television commercial for a diarrhea medication featuring a fat man in a hot tub with several friends. Someone called to him from a window, 'How's your diarrhea?' upon which the friends evacuated the tub post-haste.

'So the Bharali amoeba has reared its ugly head yet again?' she said, laughing. 'Happens every year, as soon as the temperature rises past 35 degrees Celsius. Gets into the water supply and the food chain. When anyone arrives here, they're told to take an anti-malaria pill every day and Imodium as required. Some people get their medications backwards and the result can be disastrous. I remember one poor American who had to be airlifted to Bangkok last year after taking the Imodium every day for two months. His insides were a veritable Rock of Gibraltar. By the time he saw a doctor, even his eyes had started to turn brown!'

'Yes,' added Godfrey, 'and as you know, Ambassador, the palace is the main source of intestinal terrorism. Dine with the King between April and September and you're in for a dose of Bharali bowels. He seems immune but the corps ... no diplomatic immunity there! Many of us are green around the gills, popping antibiotics like peppermints. Plays havoc with the social calendar.'

'The major topic this week was the embassy pool,' Percy explained. 'It was the usual discussion on the usual issues: who gets to use the pool; private hours for mothers and the diaper set (or not); skinny dipping after midnight (not); booze in the pool (not).'

65

What Percy was too embarrassed to tell her was that his own swimming style had also been up for discussion. He swam lengths just before lunch every day. He did the butterfly—head under water, then head up like a cork, arms flapping like windmills. Quite a sight. When he put on those goggles and launched himself, he was oblivious to everything in his path. And thus a dangerous menace, said the mothers with babies who had the shallow end of the pool reserved at the same time. The mothers put a petition to the Management Committee. They complained the ambassadorial rip tide was swamping their babies, threatening their health and safety.

'I told them the real problem in the pool is the bowel habits of the un-toilet-trained set,' he said. 'Having a reserved section of the pool for babies is like having a smoking section in a restaurant. Secondhand amoebas kill too! And then there's Piggy's dog!'

Soon after he was installed in Bharalya, Piggy had adopted one of the hundreds of street dogs which infested the capital. Lacking any human companionship himself, Piggy saw this as a huge improvement in his social life. The dog went with him to the market, to the office, and to the airport. The two were inseparable.

Dog owners are said to grow to look like their pets but Piggy and this dog were born identical twins: scrofulous, slightly drooling, rheumy eyes, huge paws flapping along the pavement, and a nose-to-the-ground navigation system. And both liked water.

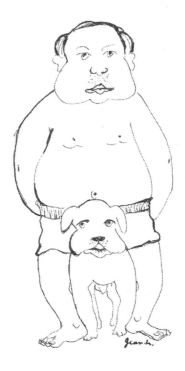

Piggy would usually arrive at the pool, dog in tow, around the same time as His Excellency. He would climb to the top of the diving tower and call out 'CANNONBALL!!!!' at the top of his lungs. Without giving anyone time to flee, he would launch his corpulence smack into the centre of the pool. The resulting tsunami not only emptied the pool but threatened to wash children, small animals, and pool furniture out to the Bay of Bengal.

One fateful day, he decided to share the pleasures of cannonballing with his dog. The two arced into the air, then hit the water simultaneously. The excitement caused the dog to lose control, as it were. So when His Excellency, arms flapping in all directions, propelled his way up the pool in the dog's slipstream, he came nose to nose with an object he never encountered in the family swimming pool in Rosedale —round, brown, glistening freshly in the sun's rays.

Percy tried to slow his momentum but, alas, too late. Ambassadorial nostrils met canine incontinence. Cacaphony! It was Percy backpedalling, adults fleeing, mothers shrieking, children crying, pool attendant sniggering. Unaware of the cause of the underwater drama unfolding, Piggy assumed Percy was drowning and dove in again to rescue him. His wake sent the offending object for the second time into Percy's horrified face.

Percy turned back to his paperwork as Godfrey and the Dragon left to continue the conversation in her office. 'All's well that ends well,' Godfrey told her. 'I put a resolution to the committee: Piggy is to be banned from the swimming pool for a month and must pay the cost of draining and cleaning the pool; the dog is to be banned for life; and an alternate venue is to be found for the ambassadorial swim. It passed unanimously.'

'What about His Excellency?' asked the Dragon.

'Well, the King has taken a shine to him. Starting tomorrow, he's invited to do his lunchtime laps at the palace pool.'

'But the amoeba …?' she protested.

'That's the price of being the ambassador,' grinned Godfrey.

෩ ෩ ෩ ෩

In the early hours of the morning after his first swim at the palace, Percy was suddenly awakened by a thunderclap of Wagnerian proportions, accompanied by bass roiling noises like the bubbling of red-hot lava deep in the earth. Half asleep, he thought the city had been struck by an earthquake or a terrorist attack.

Unfortunately for him, it was a gargantuan fart from deep within his own anatomy. His intestines were burning as if a school of piranhas were in full feeding frenzy down there. When the crater blew its top, as it were, he at last realized the horrible truth; somewhere between the fruit juice and the canapés, the dreaded Bharali amoeba had jumped ship and set up house in the ambassadorial bowel tract.

Over the next forty-eight hours, he embraced the porcelain god repeatedly as he won gold medals in every event of the intestinal Olympics.

'Is this is how my life ends?' he groaned. 'Host to the infamous Bharali amoeba?'

And not just any garden variety amoeba. The Bharali strain compared to other amoebae as King Kong did to the average chimpanzee. Biological mutation had produced a super bug combining the best features of Delhi Belly, Montezuma's Revenge, and the Tibetan Two-Step. It was rumoured that the worst fear of military planners in the Pentagon was not nuclear weapons in the hands of terrorists but this amoeba. 'A handful in the water systems of American military bases and away goes the will to fight,' they wrote in their top secret reports.

Percy was living proof. He floated between consciousness and hallucination. In his sweaty dreams, the amoeba sometimes even took on a human face—a face he knew, his nemesis and the author of his exile to Bharalya: George Crowley, Minister of Foreign Affairs.

However, thanks to those twin miracles of modern science, antibiotics and Imodium, he eventually recovered. It was the Dragon who saved the day. When she heard he was down with the trots, she rushed over to the residence, a box of pills in hand, and spoke to Marilyn in the entrance hall.

'What's happening down there?' he cried weakly from his bathroom.

'Imodium, sir,' she cried out. 'Start taking it immediately. Instant cement! Two doses and your intestines will be as solid as the Canadian Shield.'

As she went out the door, she whispered conspiratorially to Marilyn, 'Greatest human invention since Johnny Walker Black Label. Diplomacy in Bharalya would come to a halt without it.'

Christmas in Camelot

'There's no elephant available,' moaned the Dragon. 'It seems the Spanish have beaten us to it. The supplier wants to know if a camel will do. He's got two of them, a male and a female.'

'Rather unchristian of them, I say,' growled Godfrey, pacing up and down Percy's office. 'The Embassy of Canada has always had the elephant for its Christmas party. The children expect Santa to arrive on an elephant. A camel would confuse them; it would make Santa Claus look like one of the three wise men. Is there any chance at all they might get into the Christmas spirit and let us have it?'

'Not the slightest,' she replied. 'I spoke to the Spanish ambassador's social secretary and actually pleaded. She hung up on me, muttering, "Why don't you import a Canadian moose?"'

'They're still smarting over last year's shooting incident down in the Royal Game Park,' she continued. 'Nasty business it was, too; the Spanish ambassadorial buttocks were tattooed with Canadian bird-shot just as he was dropping his trousers to answer the call of nature. An accident, but it almost provoked a diplomatic note from Madrid.'

'A camel then it must be, I suppose?' asked Percy.

This was not the Dragon's first Christmas party as the ambassador's secretary and she knew a lot more than just Santa Claus was riding on this beast. 'No, sir! This means war!' she cried. 'Stern measures must be taken. Call up the Spaniards. Tell them it will be worse for them than even the Turbot War. Let them know they can say good-bye to any chance of winning the Chrysanthemum Show trophy next year if you're the judge again!'

Percy was listening to all this, uncomprehending. Elephants? Camels? Spanish-Canadian wars? Here he was in the middle of a budding diplomatic incident over—an elephant? *Is this the stuff of diplomacy here?* he wondered. His mind wandered back over the real crises he had managed in the past: trade disputes, missile crises, hijackings…

He was brought back to earth by Godfrey, encyclopedic as always in his knowledge of the insignificant, who pompously explained the geo-political importance of the party.

'The Christmas party is one of the major events of the diplomatic year. The whole diplomatic corps attends every embassy's Christmas party. It makes the ennui here almost tolerable! The Canadian party has traditionally been considered the finest in Bharalya so we are a target. Dirty tricks to unseat Canada have not been uncommon.'

'Dirty tricks?' asked a skeptical Percy.

'You can't imagine,' he replied, his eyes brightening at the memories of Yuletide disasters past. 'One year at the French Embassy party, a saboteur laced the canapés with red hot chilies; as soon as they began to eat, the entire diplomatic corps started jumping and twitching as if they had St. Vitus' dance. The children thought it was wonderful but the ambassadors were incensed. They threatened to boycott the next Bastille Day reception in reprisal. It brought the party to a messy and undignified end.'

'Surely this can't be true,' Percy sputtered. 'Sabotage, at Christmas?'

'Ask anyone. It's true. The American Embassy is one of our closest rivals and one of our most serious threats after the Spanish. We have to keep a special eye on them because we share a common garden wall. It's too easy for them to creep in unnoticed and sabotage us. They have lots of behind-the-lines Special Forces experience and believe me, they don't follow Marquis of Queensbury Rules when it comes to Christmas parties.'

The Dragon, playing tag-team with Godfrey, moved in for the *coup de grâce*. 'The Big Decision you, as ambassador, must make is: who will be Santa? Last year it was our Trade Commissioner. He was perfect. Two hundred and forty pounds, white hair, marvelous with kids, great sense of humour. Even had his own costume. Pity he was posted to another country.'

ശശശശ

A few days later, Percy called her in with Godfrey and Sylvie to resolve this major issue once and for all.

'Let's see,' he began. 'It has to be a male, fairly portly, who likes children. That means we have only a few candidates.'

'What about Georges, our security guard?' suggested Sylvie.

'Plump for sure," snorted the Dragon, 'but he refuses to take off his machine pistol. Wears it everywhere. Rumour has it he even sleeps with it between himself and his wife. Loves to fire it at any opportunity. I don't think the diplomatic corps would appreciate Santa firing a few rounds over their heads to announce his arrival, do you?'

'Well then, what about you, Godfrey?' asked Percy. 'You're about the right size.'

'Hhhmmmmf,' he grunted, vigorously shaking his head.

'I'll take that for a no. I forgot you hate children. So who's left? Pierre would be perfect but he'll be on home leave.'

Everyone thought silently. Then suddenly they looked at each other as the horrible truth dawned. As one they cried:

'But that only leaves… Omigod … Piggy!!!!!'

C3 CB CB CB

The party was in full swing when the Minister of Foreign Affairs and the Minister of Finance arrived.

The embassy grounds resonated with the voices of happy children and their parents. The diplomatic corps was present too, all dressed up in their finest. Percy's wife Marilyn was elegant in a red Christian Dior dress and matching red hat bought in London for this very occasion. Layer upon layer of silk petals wound upward from her neck; from a distance, it looked like she was wearing a red tea rose.

The garden was a riot of colour. Striped blue, red, and orange tents protected the bar and tables loaded with silver dishes from the blazing sun. Dozens of small tables covered with white tablecloths dotted the garden. And red and white Canadian flags paired with blue and green Bharali national flags fluttered in the breeze.

A huge Chinese Ferris wheel decked out in flashing Christmas lights had been rented for the day. Children screamed with delight as it lurched and creaked as if it would collapse at any moment—which apparently it once had at the Chinese Embassy, thereby prompting the Russian ambassador, in a public speech shortly after, to compare Chinese technology with the (he said) much superior Russian Ferris wheels from the Lenin Steel Works Number 6 Plant.

Yet another Sino-Russian conflict resulted. But that's another story.

Percy gave a short speech of welcome, followed by perfunctory words of congratulation from the foreign minister. 'Such a splendid party,' he droned, 'Blah-blah-blah, etc.' Unimpressed with diplomatic speeches, the children were getting restless. Marilyn made a discrete cutting gesture across her throat and Percy quickly gave the long-awaited signal.

From around the side of the embassy, a truly awesome apparition hove into view. A Bharali camel ambled into the garden, braying raucously. It was a fantastic sight, decked out in orange, yellow, and red embroidery and tiny mirrors. An unsteady humanoid clung to its hump for dear life. The humanoid in question, Piggy-Santa, jingled bells with one hand ("to create a jolly mood", he explained later from his hospital bed) and carried a sack of Christmas gifts in the other.

Human anatomy having its limitations, Piggy had no further hands to spare so the camel, not he, was the driver. He was already on the point of seasickness from just this short voyage but his 'Ship of the Desert' decided to take him on an extended tour of the garden to see what delicious camel treats might be found.

It rounded the tennis court and then suddenly stopped, its long-lashed eyes fixed directly on Marilyn's head. Slowly it started to move. Picking up speed, it headed straight to where she and the other dignitaries were seated and lurched to a stop. Then it snatched the crimson headgear in its teeth and began to munch contentedly.

Marilyn jumped up and screamed, aghast at the spectacle of her outrageously expensive hat peeking out from between the hairy lips of the beast. Several other ambassadors' wives ran over to comfort her, all the time holding their own hats well out of danger's way.

'My hat, my hat,' she cried to the ambassadors nearby. 'Catch that camel!' Alas for her, the animal was supremely dismissive of his Armani-clad herders, as if they were small dogs nipping at his legs. She watched in horror as they were knocked over in turn each time one managed to grab the bridle. The children interpreted this as a wonderful game of pin the tail on the camel.

Eventually, the camel, of its own accord, decided to rest. This pause should have provided Piggy with his chance to dismount. Unfortunately for him, just as the step ladder was being put in place, another piercing noise arose, this time from the American Embassy side of the garden wall. A second unmistakably dromedarian head poked over and let go a lovesick cry.

'Perfidious Albion!' Percy swore aloud. The Americans had *deliberately* taken the other half of the camel couple for their party, a female in heat!

He watched in disbelief as the scene unfolded as if in slow motion. The male shook off his captors one by one and, with Piggy still aboard, raced for the wall with the agility of a steeplechase champion and cleared it with ease.

Pandemonium broke out in both gardens. Children screamed. Dignitaries, too stunned to believe what they were seeing, reached for their drinks. Piggy, still holding his jingle bells but not the gifts (which now lay scattered about the lawns of two embassies) was no longer able to control his seasickness. With a wail, he demonstrated an Olympic-level capacity for projectile vomiting and splotched his lunch on the back of the American ambassador's wife several metres away. She ran screaming for the sanctuary of the house, Piggy's curry and custard meal dripping down to her ankles as she ran.

Things went downhill from there.

Up close, the picture was anything but romantic: spitting, biting, snorting, and physical contortions never attempted by the Cirque du Soleil or first-through-the-door shoppers at Sears' Boxing Day sale. Piggy-Santa, perched precariously on the back of one-half of the amorous couple, bucked and rolled like a rodeo champion, jingling all the way.

Mothers were aghast, trying to shield the eyes of their little ones from this interspecies *ménage à trois* (although Percy noted the Canadian mothers took a rather keen interest in it themselves). Piggy, suddenly religious, was imploring any and all gods to save what was left of his miserable life or end it, as the deities saw fit.

'Camels mating are not a pretty sight—or sound,' observed Godfrey. 'This experience may put me off the procreative act forever!'

The party was a disaster and guests streamed away early after offering Percy and Marilyn their condolences. When most had departed, the American ambassador and Percy surveyed the devastation: one Santa Claus hospitalized; two parties ruined; one expensive hat and an equally expensive dress destroyed. Two ambassadors consigned for the foreseeable future to their guest bedrooms.

They agreed it was time for a Christmas truce. An alliance was struck on the spot 'to get that damned elephant back next year.'

But not all was lost. On their way out, the Bharali ministers and their wives made their way to Percy and Madam to say good-bye.

'Thank you so much for inviting us to a "typical" Canadian Christmas celebration,' they said gaily. 'Wonderful party! We used to think Canadians were a bit strait-laced. We're happy to say we were wrong about you after all!'

Shakespeare Strikes Back

'I'm getting worried about the ambassador,' Godfrey said to the Dragon one day. 'He can't sleep, he can't work, he can't think about anything else. He's so obsessed with that creature. I tell you, the parrot *has* to go!'

'I fully agree,' she replied. 'Ever since his wife took in that feathered refugee from the Swedish Embassy, he's been reduced to a pitiful shadow of his former self. He comes in every morning hollow-eyed, a mad glare in his bloodshot eyes and fresh wounds on his face and hands. It's awful to behold. Things are so bad now he's afraid to open any door, whether here or at home, until someone checks whether the Evil One is inside. He even did it the other day at the Foreign Ministry. They almost called Security.'

To the uninformed observer, the parrot in question might have seemed a cute and even cuddly pet. To Percy, however, he was Beelzebub, Prince of Hell, in feathers. From the day the bird arrived, the bird had hated him. His life had become a living nightmare. He cursed the day his wife Marilyn had made her Faustian pact with the Swedish Embassy to adopt 'Shakespeare.'

His name came from his ability to recite the entire *To be or not to be* soliloquy from *Hamlet* in the plummy tones of his first owner, a former British Ambassador. He was also known to quote long verses from Edgar Allen Poe's *The Raven*:

> *Once upon a midnight dreary ...*
> *Prophet said I, thing of evil, prophet still if bird or devil ... etc.*

This added weight to Percy's certainty the bird was indeed a thing of evil.

Shakespeare was a magnificent African grey with grey plumage, a bright red tail (the Devil's colour, Percy often noted) and a razor-sharp beak ideal for amputating fingers or any other exposed part of Percy's flesh. He had been passed from embassy to embassy for a generation, and in the process had acquired an astonishing vocabulary in a dozen languages.

Shakespeare's other abilities were equally impressive. Not only could he repeat words and phrases, but he could do so in perfect intonation and the accent of the person from whom he learned them. He could do noises too. His repertoire included car engines, chain saws, microwave ovens, doors closing, and human sounds like kissing or snoring. Since coming to the Canadian Embassy, he had already learned to imitate Percy and Marilyn's voices.

Sylvie made her own unique contribution to Shakespeare's vocabulary. She delighted in teaching him some of the juicier expressions she acquired in her hometown in Gaspé. On one occasion, Shakespeare horrified visitors to the official residence by letting forth an amazing non-stop French cadenza of *Tabernac de calice d'hostie de merde* during a reception in honour of a French-speaking Member of Parliament.

Shakespeare had only one flaw: he hated men. 'The male territorial imperative,' was how Percy explained it.

To give him credit, during the first few months, Percy had made every effort to come to terms with his new lodger. When Shakespeare was alone with Marilyn, he would sit contentedly on her finger or nuzzle her neck, asking to have his feathers stroked. When her husband tried the same thing, Shakespeare let out a squawk that would perforate eardrums and latched on to the nearest available part of Percy's anatomy with his beak.

Percy in turn would scream in pain and shout, 'Oh, shit!' upon which the bird would add insult to injury by imitating Percy's cries of agony and *oh-shitting* him right back. Percy regularly came away from these encounters minus small chunks of flesh.

'It's either him or me,' Percy finally announced to Marilyn. 'One of us has to go!'

CB CB CB CB

Things finally came to a head as a result of an exchange of juicy gossip between Marilyn and Henrietta, the wife of the British ambassador, during a luncheon at the residence.

'You mean you didn't know?' she asked Marilyn over the soup. 'I thought *everyone* knew by now! It's the third time he's done it, according to my source. During their last posting, his wife returned early from a business trip and caught him *in flagrante*. She threatened to perform a little surgery if it happened again. She even keeps a small knife on the bedside table as a reminder, according to their housemaid. You know, Marilyn, you really should talk to your servants more. That's how we all learn what's really going on in the diplomatic world. Their intelligence network is fantastic, far more reliable than our MI-5 or your CSIS.'

The 'he' in question turned out to be the Belgian ambassador, Philippe Leclercq, whose European integration exercises with Sonja Andersson, the lovely wife of the Swedish chargé d'affaires, had been overheard by her cook.

Percy was not as shocked to learn this news as his wife had been, having personally observed the charms of the Swedish chargé's wife. 'I'm not surprised,' he told Marilyn. 'She's blonde, stunningly beautiful, and much younger than her husband. The Belgian ambassador's wife Valérie is very rich but she has a face like a vulture and the personality to match. Come to think of it, she and Shakespeare have a lot in common.'

'You'll have the chance to meet her soon. She visits her husband every few months when she takes time away from her law practice in Brussels. It's our turn to host the Europeans at a dinner party next month and she'll be in town.'

C3 C3 C3 C3

On the evening that sealed the fate of several guests (and one parrot), the ambassadors and their wives from France, Germany, Britain, Belgium, Sweden, Denmark, the Netherlands, and Greece were assembled around Percy's dining room table. Marilyn was closely observing the Belgian ambassador and Sonja for any sign of private communication but saw nothing. They were accompanied by their respective spouses and so were on their best official behaviour.

They had safely arrived at the salad course when the conversation turned to the latest follies of the European Parliament. It was at that point that Shakespeare flew into the room in search of human company. He looked around for a suitable landing spot and, recognizing his former mistress Sonja, perched on her shoulder. He nuzzled her affectionately. She rubbed his beak. He said a few things in Swedish. Everyone thought this was charming.

Suddenly, the bird spotted the Belgian ambassador, Philippe Leclercq. With perfect intonation, the parrot trilled to the assembled guests in Sonja's lilting voice, 'I love you, my little Belgian chocolate, I love you, Philippe.' No one in the room was in any doubt as to who was the chocolate, least of all Mme Leclercq.

But Philippe and Sonja's agony had only begun. Shakespeare then treated everyone to a repertoire of kissing sounds, finishing up with a virtuoso performance of what sounded like the track from an erotic film—with Philippe and Sonja in the leading roles! The 'oh, ohs' and 'aah, aahs' and 'don't stops' went on for several minutes.

All conversation ceased. Philippe was stunned—red-faced, open-mouthed, bug-eyed in horror. Madame Leclercq, incensed, rushed from the room, presumably to retrieve her knife.

The bird then flew to Percy's shoulder and in a perfect imitation of his voice added: 'I'm not surprised. The Belgian ambassador's wife has a face like a vulture!' and sunk his beak into Percy's ear.

There were two distinctly different reactions around the table: shock on the part of the Swedes and Belgians, and laughter on the part of everyone else. Everyone else that is, except Percy, who ran from the room bleeding profusely, vowing revenge.

Things eventually returned to normal at the residence. Marilyn reflected carefully on the matter and concluded (in a close decision) that it was Shakespeare, not Percy, who had to go.

Madame Leclercq returned to Brussels and sued her former husband for all his worldly possessions and pension. Happily for him, she decided surgery was not worth the trouble and left the knife, unused, in the family bedroom.

The Swedish chargé and Sonja reconciled, on condition that Shakespeare was never heard from again in their presence.

As for Shakespeare, no one knows his fate, except Percy and his cook. And like any good members of an embassy's staff, they're not telling.

I've Got a Lov-er-ly Bunch of Coconuts

'It must be a great honour being the Consul of Canada,' Sylvie said to Godfrey one day. To her mind, 'consul' conjured up images of ancient Rome where becoming consul was the career goal of every politician. Mind you, she also remembered from school that Caligula, one of the crazier emperors, wanted to name his favourite horse to the post of consul. But she didn't think it politic to mention *that* to Godfrey.

Godfrey missed the irony and rose to the bait. 'It's a royal pain,' he muttered, stirring his coffee faster and faster in his frustration. 'Look at those damned lost passport applications on my desk. Five of them this week alone! All lost because people can't keep track of their own belongings. The moment they get outside Canada, they lose their luggage and their wits. They imagine the embassy will get them out of any jam.'

'Surely some of the work is interesting, isn't it, Godfrey?'

'No,' he snapped. 'Here's what else I have to cope with. Just yesterday, two characters turned up at my office. They were travelling from Bharalya to Thailand on unicycles, *unicycles* if you please! The big-wheeled kind you see in the circus. Extraordinary! One apparently fell off and broke his collarbone. When they went for medical help, somebody stole his cycle. I'm not the bloody Lost and Found!'

She tried to interrupt him but too late. He was already launched into a rant.

'I get them all. Defrocked missionaries. Stranded tourists. Relatives of disappeared persons. Kids in prison for trying to smuggle drugs from Myanmar through here. The Bharalis aren't amused by that, by the way. They have signs at the airport saying drug smuggling is punishable by death and they mean it.'

He then jumped up, waving his hands wildly. 'Of course, when the country blows up, we really have a time of it. Have to locate every damn Canadian and get them evacuated. Many never register with us and it's the devil's own job to find them when their families back home start to panic. Quite a number don't want to be found at all and give us a hard time. Does anyone ever thank us for what we do?'

Sylvie was not about to answer.

'Not on your Nelly. If you want to learn about people, consular affairs is the best university in the world. By the way, I see from the schedule you're duty officer next week. Good luck.'

'Next week?' she asked blankly.

'I guess they forgot to tell you. Somebody must always be on consular duty and it's your turn next week. It's up to you to sort out whatever comes up. And, oh, by the way, here's the most important thing you need to know: the Godfrey Sutherland-Jones Rule Number One. Don't *ever* call me at home.'

C3 C3 C3 CB

The dreaded call came at midnight. She was just falling asleep after practicing some Bharali phrases she had learned that day.

'This is the Airport Night Manager, Lufthansa Airlines. We have a 737 sitting on the tarmac with one hundred and thirty-three passengers on board. One of them is a Canadian and he refuses to put on any clothes. We can't take off until he does. What are you going to do about it?'

'I'll be right there,' she heard herself say confidently. 'I'll take care of it.'

The moment she put the phone down, the reality of what she had just said hit her. *Take care of it? Merde!* she thought. *I haven't the faintest idea what I'm going to do.*

All she knew was that whatever she did, there would be a hundred and thirty-three plus people watching her do it. Her fifteen minutes of fame—her consular moment—had arrived.

She dressed quickly and reached into her husband's closet for some masculine clothes—just in case. Only later did she discover they were his favourite pants and jacket. The duty car whisked her through the darkened city and fifteen minutes later, the bright lights of the airport came into view.

Her arrival in the terminal was greeted with the expectant awe usually accorded to the police or firemen first on the scene of a disaster. The building was deserted, except for the Lufthansa desk. Just a few souls were milling about there—airline personnel, police, and a few families who had come to see their loved ones off to Europe. Shouts and accusations in English and German echoed though the waiting area. Unfortunately, she was able to understand both.

'Crazy fool. Thinks he's some sort of guru!' was the English language theme. The Germans had a more nationalistic reaction. 'This plane will be late. The efficiency of the airline is at stake. We will be the laughing stock of Europe. People will compare us with Mongolian Airlines. Or worse, Air Canada!'

She pressed on through the terminal to the tarmac and eventually climbed up the steps into the plane, carrying her husband's jacket and pants.

She spotted her fellow countryman right away. There he was, meditating on his seat in the lotus position, clad only in a saffron loincloth. He had a beatific, slightly spaced out smile on his face. On the floor in front of him was a string bag full of coconuts.

Even before they spoke, one thing was immediately clear. He had successfully avoided contact with soap or water for a long, no, a *very* long, time. His seatmate, a large middle-aged German businessman, had his face pressed against the window, blue from holding his breath.

Flashing her consular ID card, she introduced herself in her most official tone: 'Consul, Canadian Embassy.' Her mother would have been impressed. She herself was impressed. Unfortunately, neither the businessman nor the guru was.

Playing for time, she asked the businessman, now gasping for air like a freshly landed mackerel, if he would mind moving to the empty seat she had spotted near the front of the plane. Leapfrogging the guru with a speed belying his Teutonic bulk, he set an Olympic record as he raced toward the front. She heard the German words for 'smelly', 'goat,' and 'Canadian' as he wheezed his way up the aisle.

Gradually her client's story began to take shape.

'I'm from New Brunswick, I'm twenty-five and I'm totally broke,' he explained. 'I've spent the last year walking around India to find myself. What I learned during a revelation on the road to Darjeeling was that I was a holy man in an earlier incarnation. There and then I decided to give up all my worldly goods for a religious life.'

And the fleshpots of Moncton, Sylvie wondered?

'Unfortunately, I also discovered not all human beings are kind; I was beaten and robbed and I acquired many intestinal bugs too. So this week I came to the embassy for help.'

Sylvie could just imagine the scene: the unwashed guru cross-legged on Godfrey's pristine red leather sofa, and Godfrey simultaneously looking down his nose and holding it.

'I don't understand what all the fuss is about,' he insisted. 'I'm dressed like any other holy man.'

Sylvie was flummoxed. He did not agree to leave the plane or to get dressed — even if he possessed clothes. Which, he said, he did not. One hundred and thirty-three passengers and several unhappy German flight attendants watched her every move, more impatient with every passing minute. Three large Bharali security men were waiting to spring into action.

Her moment of truth had arrived. Suddenly, she knew what to do.

Looking him in the eye she said, 'As a holy man, you understand charity. I am a religious person myself; I understand about giving alms. I have a gift for you. Please accept these clothes as a token of the esteem and respect of the consul of Canada.'

He reflected on this for a moment. Slowly, he unwound himself from his yoga position, put on the jacket, then the pants and finally, taking her hand, said softly, 'The consul is most kind. Please accept in return the only thing I have in this world—this lovely bunch of coconuts.'

Management by Results

'Oh, dear,' said Godfrey. 'It looks like Ottawa is going through yet another spasm of Management-itis.'

Godfrey had his feet on his desk, his favourite position when absorbing unpleasant news. 'This announcement to the whole Department of Foreign Affairs says we are all now to bow down to a new god: Accountability. We haven't even finished worshipping Management by Results, last year's hot new deity. Or Modern Comptrollership and Values and Ethics, who joined the pantheon only a few years before! It doesn't tell us if this new religion is monotheistic, meaning we have to kick out the previous gods, or whether we can simply worship the whole lot of them as a sort of a theological smorgasbord! Very confusing for us humble diplomats.'

'Yes, yes, Godfrey, but what do we have to *do*?' asked Percy.

'*Do*? Oh, absolutely nothing,' he replied, clearly surprised at the question. Seeing the puzzled expression on Percy's face—a former assistant deputy minister who imagined a directive from above might imply having to obey—Godfrey shared the wisdom that had served him well over thirty years in the foreign service. 'I subscribe to the *King Solomon's Mines* school of management. Everything I ever needed to know about management, I learned from that book. Do you remember the story?'

'Yes, of course, the H. Rider Haggard story. But I don't see the link.'

'Two intrepid English explorers arrive in Africa to find King Solomon's legendary mines and steal the diamonds. They try to put one over on the local king by claiming they're gods from the heavens. The king's witch doctor says, "Prove it," so they threaten to make the moon go dark. They know from reading their farmer's almanac there will be an eclipse but of course, they don't tell the king that. The witch doctor knows the king is being taken for a ride and she tries to warn him, crying out as the moon darkens, "It will pass; I have seen this before." Unfortunately for him, the king doesn't listen and believes the explorers. Result: He loses his kingdom and his mines. Those explorers were the direct ancestors of today's management gurus. Now they carry laptops instead of almanacs but the con's the same.'

'And the moral of the story is?'

'Don't get excited. This too shall pass.'

'Well, not quite yet, I'm afraid, Godfrey. We are about to get a visit from the guru of Modern Management herself, the departmental Inspector General. She's coming out from Ottawa for a week to find out what we're doing wrong and report back to the deputy minister.'

'*Wrong,* of course, doesn't necessarily mean *bad,*' protested Godfrey. 'It just means *not in line with the latest management fad.* I'll bet she's out to convert us or kill us, just like the missionaries or the Grand Inquisitor; you confess or she gets out the hot irons and the thumbscrews. I've heard she threatens those who resist with a quick posting back to headquarters. Even if we survive that, it will double our paperwork and mean hiring another accountant. We'll also have to put the *accountability* buzzword into every document we write. Until the next buzzword arrives.'

'Frank will bear the brunt but he's been through this many times before,' Percy declared confidently. 'The Inspector General is no match for Frank.'

Frank Kobayashi, the embassy administrative officer, was a former naval officer who had served in a variety of difficult countries around the world. He was short and bald but tough, street-smart, and completely hostile to bureaucracy. Auditors were his least favourite sub-species. He was alleged to have said to the last one, 'An auditor is someone who doesn't know how to cook but drives their spouse crazy by reorganizing the kitchen.'

Frank ran things by the 'informal' methods generally used in Bharalya—favours and cash transactions—which would have driven Treasury Board officials in Ottawa wild, had they known about them. Which Frank prayed they never would. He kept a second set of books and rumour had it they were much more reliable than the official embassy accounts. This was general knowledge but every ambassador knew Frank did nothing for his own benefit. That is why none of them ever inquired too closely about how he got things done.

He was the real power in the place; the ambassador could do nothing without his okay. He had a network of friends and operatives at all levels in Bharali society including his good drinking buddy, the chief of police.

C3 C3 C3 C3

A few weeks later, the Inspector General arrived. Godfrey returned pale and sweating after his first meeting with her. He came into Percy's office for moral support.

'What's she like?' Percy asked.

'Grey hair, grey eyes, grey suit, grey platinum-rimmed glasses. She's a no-nonsense, steely-eyed accountant who delights in finding wrongdoing everywhere, real or imagined. If she was stopped on the street by a beggar, she'd likely lecture him on how to re-engineer his business processes. She's a professional auditor, one of the new breed,' he added. 'Sees herself as a crusader. She really *believes* the world's problems can be fixed with Modern Management. She has a model in her laptop and if we don't fit inside it, she'll happily cut off any bits sticking out. Even Frank's going to find her a challenge, I'm afraid.'

'Has she ever travelled to Asia before?' asked Percy.

'Never. Said she considers travelling an inefficient use of her time.'

'Oh, dear,' groaned Percy. 'Good luck to us all.'

The next week was frenetic for the whole embassy and especially for Frank. The Inspector General set up headquarters in the office next to his and for twelve hours a day, carried out a military-style investigation of every facet of the embassy's operations. The door to her office was constantly in motion with people coming in carrying files, documents, and strong coffee. By the end of the week, she had everything in her computer and demanded to see the ambassador and Frank at zero eight hundred hours, sharp.

When they met her, they couldn't decide whether she was on the verge of an orgasm or a cardiac event. They thought she might faint, she looked so distraught. 'Let me tell you,' Frank regaled everyone later, 'an emotional accountant is a terrible thing to behold.'

'Ambassador,' she began, 'I am shocked. I have never seen anything like this in all my life. Treasury Board and the Auditor General,' she added, genuflecting slightly, 'will hear about this.' Finally, looking Percy and Frank in the eye, she delivered her favourite line: 'There will be Drastic Consequences for you both!'

With that, she stopped for breath, panting like a horse at the end of the Queen's Plate.

Percy suspected she would have preferred drawing and quartering, but being modern, would settle for a simple execution by injection. Frank saw his future counting paper clips in a cubicle in the basement filing room at headquarters.

To calm her down, Percy asked whether she would agree to have dinner with Marilyn and himself that evening, her last in Bharalya. She accepted, but only after pausing to convince herself this would not contradict any conflict of interest regulations.

Thanks to a couple of bracing martinis and some excellent Bordeaux, she even seemed to enjoy herself—at least as much as an auditor can. This gave Percy the opening to propose a small tour of the city the following day before her evening flight.

CB CB CB CB

Godfrey and Frank ran into her by chance around noon the following day, just as she was returning to the embassy from her tour. She was not the same woman. She was now hysterical and clearly in shock. *She probably just could not cope with the disorder*, Godfrey first thought. *Culture shock. The streets, the beggars, the animals, the crush of people, the noise, the chaos—all outside her normal frame of reference.*

But soon they learned there was more to it than that. While she was touring, her hotel room had been robbed and 'stripped bare', she told them. Everything was gone: her clothes, her passport, and, most important of all, her laptop computer with all their sins recorded in it.

'DO SOMETHING!!' she screeched. And then suddenly breaking into tears, she sobbed, 'What am I going to do?'

This was Frank's finest moment.

Giving her his handkerchief, he patted her shoulder sympathetically. 'We will do everything we can. We can issue you a new passport but I'm afraid your clothes and computer will be on sale in the bazaar before the day is over.'

'You could make a formal complaint to the police,' added Godfrey, 'but I advise against it. They will have your visa cancelled to prevent you leaving the country. Under Bharali law, you are required to identify your belongings in person if the thief is caught. You could end up spending weeks here.'

'Worse than that,' continued Frank, 'the police will expect an *incentive* to speed up the proceedings, if you know what I mean. The price can be steep. You of all people can't charge that to your Treasury Board travel expenses, can you? In the unlikely event they do find your belongings, they will remain in police custody as evidence until the trial is over. You will need to hire a local lawyer too. We can provide you with a list of names. And of course, you will have to return here and stay for the entire trial.'

'How long is that likely to take?' she gasped, now in even deeper shock as the reality of her situation sunk in.

'Between two and five years,' said Frank, turning away to hide his smile.

She looked at Frank beseechingly. 'Is there anything you can do?' she pleaded. 'Anything?'

Frank paused for effect.

'Well,' he said, 'there is perhaps another option. Robberies at that hotel are not unknown. The police can likely guess who the thief was. It would not be too hard for them to find your things either, I expect; this is a rather small city after all. The chief of police is a drinking pal of mine but he has an unfortunate problem. He loves good Scotch but there are only two ways to get it here: from a diplomat, which is counter to'—he paused for effect again—'Treasury Board regulations; or on the black market, where the price is exorbitant. It's well beyond the pitiful salary he's paid by his government. What I am saying is, you *could* have your computer back in time for your flight, if …'

The Inspector General slowly regained her composure and managed to croak out, 'You mean …?'

'Yes,' he replied. 'You see, madam, everything in Bharalya has a price. That's the way the system works here. I think two cases of Johnny Walker Black Label to the chief should do it.'

Her first reaction was outrage, her second, despair. Her shifting emotions played out in her eyes. Seeing her soften slightly, Frank delivered his final line like an orchestra conductor ending a symphony. 'Think of it this way, madam. It will cost you less than the value of your computer. It's the most *efficient* solution.'

The struggle was over. She grabbed on to the word *efficient* (one of her favourite words) as a drowning woman clings to a life preserver. 'Yes,' she said brightening suddenly. 'That's it. It's the most *efficient* solution!'

'There is one other little thing you'll have to do, however.'

'Whatever you say. Of course.'

'The chief of police would be extremely unhappy if I were to lose my job. A critical report on the embassy would also be bad for him. It might even lead to the government closing it down.'

'You mean you want me to … to …?' she screeched, aghast.

'Exactly,' he calmly replied. 'When in Rome, Madam …"

War and Peace

'Boredom is the root of all evil,' Godfrey declared in a solemn voice. He had his feet on his desk and a book in his hands. Percy backed quickly toward the door. When Godfrey waxed philosophical, he made everyone feel the world was on the point of ending and suicide was the only option. But Percy was not to escape.

'Ambassador, the ultimate tendency of civilization is toward barbarism. Just consider the diplomatic corps in this country. Look at what happened at the King's summer palace last year.'

Having failed to escape, Percy chose a comfortable chair and Godfrey warmed to his tale of diplomat's inhumanity to diplomat.

'Every year the King invites the diplomatic corps up to his summer palace in the mountains. It's the last major event on the diplomatic calendar, a few weeks before everyone goes home on leave. The idea is to give us a taste of the country beyond the capital. It's rather like the annual Arctic trip Canada used to offer foreign ambassadors. Here in Bharalya it's not polar bears and ice-breakers, though. It's a long weekend of golf in the mountains. His Majesty gives a silver trophy for the winning golf foursome and the French Embassy throws in a case of Mouton Rothschild.'

'Sounds idyllic.'

'Oh, no, just the contrary. It's more like Dante's inner circle. It brings out the worst in human character. Several embassies have not spoken to each other since.'

Why this particular weekend should be top of mind for Godfrey was soon clear. He had learned from the Dragon that Percy had that very morning received the embassy's invitation to this year's event. Godfrey was determined to persuade him to decline. To no avail, as it turned out, despite a heroic lobbying effort which would have made Karlheinz Schreiber proud.

'Those who do not learn from history are condemned to repeat it!' he finally muttered and turned back to his book, the biography of Niccolò Machiavelli.

C3 C3 C3 C3

And so it was that in late May, Percy, Madam, and their senior staff arrived at the gates of His Majesty's summer palace for a weekend of diplomatic fun and games.

The scene was spectacular. The palace was set in a high valley surrounded by stands of ancient pine. It was built by His Majesty's grandfather in the 1920s on a scale unimaginable today, in white marble and pink granite. It looked out over a private lake against a backdrop of towering snow-capped Himalayan peaks. That day, the cloudless blue sky shimmered in the clear mountain air. The lawns were emerald green and perfectly manicured. Percy and Marilyn could make out peacocks strutting on the grass in their blue-green plumage. It was paradise, Bharalya's answer to Banff but without the tourists.

His Majesty's chief of protocol welcomed everyone and went over the program.

'Ambassadors who are so inclined will play golf on Saturday and Sunday while the rest of the diplomatic corps do whatever they please. Saturday evening, the king will arrive, and dinner will be served on our traditional Bharali boats. There will be musical entertainment too. To conclude the evening, His Majesty's yacht will lead the regatta around the small island in the middle of the lake. Prizes for the winning golf foursome will be awarded jointly by His Majesty and the French ambassador on Sunday afternoon. I hope you will enjoy your weekend.'

C3 C3 C3 C3

The first evening, the atmosphere on the patio was relaxed. Diplomats and their spouses chatted amiably. Good food and wine created a mood of almost pastoral harmony. Even the ever-present risk of being laid low by the Bharali amoeba seemed forgotten.

The following morning, the opening round of golf began peacefully as well. Every embassy turned out and there was much laughter and good-natured joking as they teed off.

As the morning wore on, however, two foursomes clearly emerged as the front-runners. The Latin Bloc, grouping together Spain, Mexico, Argentina, and Chile, had a brilliant first nine holes and pulled well ahead of the pack. The Anglo-Saxon Alliance of Britain, Canada, Australia, and New Zealand played almost as well, although they were handicapped by a language barrier; neither Britain nor Canada could understand a word said by Australia, so New Zealand was pressed into service as interpreter.

Many countries were on the course that day but the Italians stood out for special mention. They couldn't agree who should be their partners; they spent hours arguing and shouting among themselves until they eventually noticed everyone else had gone. They never teed off at all.

When Their Excellencies returned after the first eighteen holes, the atmosphere was considerably less congenial than the evening before. The facial expressions of the Anglo-Saxons and the Sino-Russo-Franco-American Alliance in particular were set and determined. One could see national pride was now at stake. The British ambassador was giving his allies a pep talk for tomorrow in which the words 'Long live the British Empire!' were spoken, only partly in jest.

As for the Latins, they were buoyant and happy, pleased with their performance. But something had changed for them too. This was becoming an affair of honour, awakening the ghosts of past defeats in the Old and New Worlds. 'Remember the Falkland Islands!' they shouted as they toasted their success of the day.

Dinner on the boats was a formal affair, black ties and long dresses. Outwardly, the scene was one of elegance, an aristocratic tableau worthy of the London court of King George I. Dinner conversation flowed easily, perhaps because so much alcohol was consumed. The Russian boat in particular swayed dangerously as its diplomats repeatedly jumped to their feet to toast their homeland in duty-free vodka.

Things started to go seriously wrong when the boats drew up behind His Majesty's yacht for the naval procession. It all began with some seemingly innocent bumping. The Spanish boat collided 'accidentally' with the Russian just as another toast to Mother Russia was in progress. The entire Russian contingent, the ambassador included, spilled into the lake.

At that very moment, the British had been attempting to block the Spanish boat from the other side when they themselves were bumped by the Argentineans. After that, it was difficult to say who did what to whom. At some point, an English voice—possibly the Military Attaché—called out in the dark, 'Sink the Armada!' and the Spanish boat mysteriously capsized and sank. The bedraggled Spanish ambassador and his party had to swim to shore in their evening wear. Not a pretty sight.

Oblivious to the debacle unfolding behind him, His Majesty Sasha II, Slayer of the Elephant, sailed forward triumphantly in full regalia, accompanied by Handel's *Water Music* and a gigantic display of fireworks. In the King's mind, this *was* London and he *was* George I. It was only when his yacht rounded the island that he noticed no one was following and that two of the boats in his procession had already overturned.

The scene on shore was not one of international goodwill. As Godfrey would have said, being dumped into the water in black tie does not bring out the best in diplomats. Everyone claimed everyone else had acted maliciously. Some even said aloud they believed it was all planned in advance, a ploy to gain advantage in the golf match the following day.

Needless to say, the second round of golf the next morning degenerated into something closer to war than sport. It was marked by ugly incidents and dirty tricks; balls were mysteriously kicked from the greens into the rough and favourite clubs went missing. When the Spanish ambassador was about to putt on the final hole, someone shot a ball directly at him and registered a painful (for him) hole in one. Scoring was especially suspicious; never in the history of the royal tournament had so many birdies been miraculously achieved on the back nine—and all by the Sino-Russo-Franco-American foursome!

The chief of protocol tried to restore order but to no avail. In the end, the King had no option but to declare it was impossible to name a winner and announced the cup would not be awarded. Every embassy was unhappy and the weekend broke up in mutual recrimination. It was not the diplomatic corps' finest hour.

CR CR CR CR

Back at the embassy on Monday morning, Percy went to see Godfrey with some trepidation. And with good reason. Before he could say a word, Godfrey looked up from his papers and smiled condescendingly like a father upon his prodigal son.

'I did warn you, you know, Ambassador. Civilization is a very thin veneer indeed.'

National Daze

'What do you all think about the latest policy announcement from George Crowley?' Godfrey asked his colleagues.

'Another helpful directive from our favourite minister,' said Pierre sarcastically. 'He already has the record, but this time this time he has surpassed himself.'

'You mean the embassy won't be celebrating Canada Day this year at all?' asked a horrified Sylvie. 'That's impossible, surely.'

'Actually, it could be a blessing in disguise,' Godfrey said, chuckling. 'For once we'll have a nice quiet July 1 without the diplomatic corps tromping through our flower beds and sucking up our Scotch in the name of patriotism.'

'Wait a minute,' said Pierre, 'Ottawa doesn't say we *have* to cancel, they just tell us they have no money in the budget for Canada Day receptions and dinners. It seems the department overspent its flag budget and has to cut back elsewhere, but they have millions of Canadian flags in stock. They've offered to send us a thousand of the damned things if we just ask. What are they thinking? People don't come to national day parties for flags—they come for the free booze!'

'But I also read in that message the minister says we are allowed to raise money, if we want to,' Sylvie protested.

'Marvelous!' Godfrey sneered. 'What does he think we're going to do? Hold bake sales? Rent out the ambassador's limo for weddings and funerals?'

Percy so far had said nothing. He was certainly not in agreement with Godfrey. In his view, hosting a national day party was one of the very few useful functions of the diplomatic corps in Bharalya.

'It matters,' he finally said in a serious tone, 'to showcase Canada to the world. We don't have much visibility here so I want this to be a blockbuster celebration. We simply *must* raise the money. Every other embassy seems to manage a national day reception despite the international economic downturn. Maybe we can learn something from them.'

೮೩ ೮೩ ೮೩ ೮೩

The following week, during a luncheon at the Swedish embassy, there was a conversation about national days. 'What are your countries doing this year?' Percy asked casually. 'Is anyone planning to cancel?'

The French ambassador looked at Percy, uncomprehending. *'Annuler? Mais non! Quelle idée!* Bastille Day is not only for France but for the entire world! This year we intend to build a model of the Eiffel Tower on the embassy grounds. Singers and musicians are coming from the Opéra de Paris and we will have wines, cheeses, and foie gras flown in specially. At midnight we will have a magnificent display of fireworks which will so impress the Bharali foreign minister and the king, they will rush to join La Francophonie this year. And I will use the occasion to announce a new direct weekly Air France flight between Paris and Bharalya.'

The Chinese ambassador was no less surprised by the question. 'China intends to celebrate our national day by bringing the great People's Liberation Army Band to play at the royal palace. I will announce a major gift of military hardware including fighter planes and helicopters plus a new road through the Himalayas linking our two countries.' He added with pride, 'It will be an engineering wonder of the world.'

India, not to be outdone by China, would be showcasing its economic ties. A major business delegation would be there for its Independence Day celebration, and a signing ceremony was planned to make official dozens of new Indian investments in the manufacturing and energy sectors.

The United States and Russia had similarly grand plans for their respective days. The centrepiece for each was to be the announcement of a new military base in the country.

Nicely neutralizing both sides, thought Percy. *His Majesty is a clever negotiator.*

Before anyone could ask the inevitable question about Canada's intentions, Percy deftly complimented their host on the excellent quality of the wine, and returned the conversation to the usual subjects—food, wine, and golf.

After the lunch, the Swedish chargé d'affaires took him aside for a moment and said, 'I hear by the grapevine your foreign ministry is going through another round of cutbacks too. Not to worry. We've faced them for the past few years. So have the Danes, the Norwegians, and the Finns. Most of the other small embassies here have, but they all found ways to keep up appearances and put on a big national day show.'

'What's your secret?' asked Percy, intrigued.

'I'll give it to you in two words: *fundraising*—not easily done. And *sponsorships*—you put the arm on somebody else to pay the bills. Our national day this year will be entirely paid for by IKEA.'

CဒCဒCဒCဒ

With this idea dancing in his head, Percy convened the embassy management committee next morning and tried it out on his incredulous staff.

'Fundraising? Sponsorships? You're not serious,' said Godfrey. 'You mean, selling off bits of the Canada Day party to the highest bidder? I can see it now: Would you care for a canapé, Your Majesty? The arctic char is brought to you by Botulism Bay Fish Packers and the biscuits are donated by Bulimia Bakeries.'

Sylvie was equally horrified but more practical in her response. '*Hostie*! Who in Canada is going to sponsor a reception ten thousand miles away in this part of the world?'

Percy cut off discussion at this point. 'Colleagues, if you think this is tough, let me tell you what the government is planning to do in Ottawa. The Canada Day celebration this year will be replaced by an hour-long television speech by the Prime Minister. He'll talk stone-faced about the joys of frugality and his latest belt-tightening measures.'

'So, old party-pooper will depress us yet again?'

'That's right. He'll say he has already asked the Governor General to lead by example. Visitors to Rideau Hall will be asked to bring a food donation as the price of admission, to defray the costs of all those revenue-draining dinners for visiting heads of state, war heroes, and Order of Canada recipients. The grounds will be converted into "Rideau Market Gardens". Surplus produce will be sold by the sentries in full regalia at the guardhouse—er, food stall—at the front gate.'

'Noooo.'

'Yes. And it gets better. Government offices in Ottawa will be told to turn themselves into profit centres. Do you remember those containers with decorative greenery on the balcony around the ninth floor of foreign affairs headquarters, where the diplomatic dining rooms are? They'll be replaced with pots of *fines herbes* and vegetables. Public buildings throughout Ottawa will have to sprout rooftop gardens too. Those costly rubber plants and decorative figs in cubicle-land will be replaced by hydroponic vegetables and miniature fruit trees. Public servants will have to use their coffee breaks to weed and prune. And on Saturday mornings during harvest season, deputy ministers will be at their stands in the farmers' market.

'So you see,' he concluded, 'I'm afraid we have no option. You're in charge, Godfrey. You can ask Piggy to help you, if you like. Fundraising or sponsorships. Your choice.' And then, without thinking, he added the fateful words, 'It doesn't matter where you find the money, as long as you find it.'

Those two were normally the last persons one would put in charge of a happy social event but Percy optimistically felt things would turn out all right. It was only a Canada Day party, after all.

C3 C3 C3 C3

Late in June, the embassy awoke from its drowsy summer torpor. Lawns and flowerbeds were suddenly filled with people hard at work. The same gardeners who normally passed their days moving plants from one flowerbed to another and slowly back again in, as Godfrey often described it, 'a masterful imitation of working,' were actually doing work. Grass was really being mowed and bushes trimmed.

Workmen appeared from everywhere carrying scaffolding, tents, tables, and chairs. Coloured lights were strung up. An orchestra platform was erected at the rear of the garden. Boxes of china, glassware, and cutlery, and napkins bearing the Canadian maple leaf logo were delivered under Frank's watchful eye. No theft could escape his notice; anyone daring to try would risk banishment from future employment, if not also an interview with his close friend, the chief of police.

Godfrey and Piggy were unusually tight-lipped about the event's source of funding. All they would say was that they had indeed found a way and it would be a surprise. Everyone would find out on July 1.

When that day finally arrived, everything was ready. Marilyn and Percy were at the front door to welcome the Bharali foreign minister and his wife. Soon all the other guests followed, the ever-present diplomatic corps and the two hundred or so Canadians living in Bharalya. For the occasion, Marilyn was splendorous in a white, flowery hat of sufficient girth to cast a shadow on people standing a metre on each side of her. Percy was decked out in a white linen suit and sported a large maple leaf pin in the lapel.

He was overheard to say to the minister in greeting, 'I realize you attend so many national day celebrations, Minister, but I think you'll come away from this one feeling Canada's is unique and original.'

'I already have that sense,' the foreign minister replied non-committally. Percy looked puzzled, certain he had misheard, but the strains of the orchestra playing in the garden put the obvious follow-up question out of his mind.

The sun was just beginning to set. Brightly hued tents and twinkling lights lent the garden a festive air. Tables had been arranged tastefully and set with the embassy's finest dishes. At several points, bars had been set up with bottles and glasses. At the front of the garden stood a microphone flanked by two Canadian flags.

Percy moved to it quickly and pulled out his Canada Day speech. He waxed eloquent about what a proud, independent country Canada was, northern, strong, and free, and how its national symbols, the beaver and the Royal Canadian Mounted Police, symbolized Canada's love of industry and good government.

Polite applause followed but stopped abruptly when a pimply, tattooed teenager suddenly shouted out from the back row, 'Hey dude, how come you're passing the collection plate this year?'

'Yeah,' echoed the wife of a Canadian businessman, 'how come we couldn't get in without paying?'

'Do we have to pay for parking too?' chimed in a third.

The entire diplomatic corps and the Bharali minister and his wife pretended they were not there, eyes focused on a non-existent object up in the sky. The Swedish chargé d'affaires shook his head. Percy stood speechless, mortified by the questions. He prayed this was only a bad dream but he couldn't seem to wake up.

'Have a look for yourself at the front gate,' cried yet another attendee. 'You should be ashamed.'

With that, Percy took Marilyn by the arm and the two walked quickly to the front gate to see what everyone was talking about. There, right next to the crested gates, they were confronted with what looked like a ticket booth and a huge billboard bearing the official coat of arms of the Government of Canada.

Percy gasped as he read:

WELCOME TO THE CANADA COUNTRY CLUB AND EMBASSY. MONTHLY MEMBERSHIPS NOW ON SALE. PLEASE ALSO NOTE GEORGE CROWLEY, MINISTER OF FOREIGN AFFAIRS OF CANADA, HAS DECREED ALL DIPLOMATIC PARTIES ARE NOW ON A COST-RECOVERY BASIS. A CONVENIENT BOX HAS BEEN SET UP AT THE FRONT GATES FOR YOUR CASH DONATIONS. PLEASE GIVE GENEROUSLY.

The guests were soon treated to the rare spectacle of an ambassador in full gallop in hot pursuit of two of his own diplomats. Piggy was running for his life with Godfrey not far behind. As the three disappeared out of sight into the parking lot, Percy's words were definitely not ones usually heard in a diplomatic setting. 'When I get my hands on you, you idiots …' was the last thing the guests heard.

ଓଃ ଓଃ ଓଃ ଓଃ

But the story did not end there. When the embassy accounts were forwarded to Ottawa, Percy received an unexpected message from the deputy minister herself. He was astounded to read that he had been named Most Innovative Ambassador of the Year for his creative financing of Canada Day and for discovering a lucrative new stream of revenue.

He was even more gobsmacked to learn that George Crowley had heard about it and immediately instructed all embassies to follow Bharalya's lead. They were given just one year to convert their facilities to country clubs and timeshares.

The government also announced its intent to enter negotiations with Club Med to take over responsibility for management of all Canadian embassies. Rumour has it the new chain will be called 'Club Dip'.

All's Well that Ends Well

The dreaded call from Ottawa came just before noon. For weeks, rumours of the impending closure of the embassy had been rampant. When the red telephone rang, the Dragon literally jumped, she was so nervous. Percy took the call with his usual calm.

'Ambassador Williamson? Please stay on the line. The deputy minister will speak with you now.'

The Dragon tiptoed back to her office. Percy would tell her all later.

'Percy, Suzanne de Varennes here. I'm just calling to give you a heads up. Your good friend, the minister, has got it into his head he wants to announce another Bold New Foreign Policy before the next election. As you know, that's the fourth BNFP we've had in four years. Nobody in the G-8 has any idea what Canada will do next. We're becoming a laughing stock, the Three Stooges of the international community.'

'Yes, I've noticed.'

'It gets worse. The Minister for International Cooperation has caught the same virus. It must be contagious. She wants to close down all the aid programs in your region to focus instead on Central America. Goodness knows what we'd actually do there. We've already had six different priorities in five years—first it was environment, then infrastructure, then agriculture, then good governance, then women and children, and now, solar energy and windmills! Of course, all that doesn't matter. It's really about wooing the voters next time around.'

'Politics trumps policy again, eh?'

'Exactly.'

'And let me guess,' Percy said sadly, 'you're calling to tell me Bharalya is one of the aid programs on her hit list, right?'

'Worse than that, my friend. Minister Crowley wants to close the embassy down completely, sell off the assets, and pack most of you off to early retirement.'

There was a long pause. The deputy minister heard a sharp intake of breath.

'But what about the oil drilling contract? That's why the embassy is still open, according to the minister.'

'Signed this morning in Calgary, Percy. The deal is done. That's why he's now ready to move ahead with closing. We've got less than a month before this goes to Cabinet for decision. I just wanted to keep you informed.'

'Can I share any of this with the Bharalis?'

'Yes, but off the record.'

'Click' went the red phone.

Percy sat quietly for a while, considering what to do. He remembered what Marilyn once said about the role of an ambassador:

> *An ambassador is not the person sent abroad to lie for his or her country. No, an ambassador is the poor schmuck caught between the host country (the rock) and his or her own government (the hard place). Casualties from friendly fire vastly outnumber those killed in battle.*

He got up from his desk and gazed out his window at the palm trees, totally still under the blazing tropical sun. The Dragon will be fine, he reflected, but what about Godfrey? Frank? Piggy? All the loyal Bharali staff? Marilyn and myself? So many people hurt and for no good policy reason.

Not this time, he finally decided. He flexed his muscles and said in the direction of the telephone, 'George, enough is enough. Now it's my turn.'

ᏆᏆᏆᏆ

Meanwhile, in the King's private office, several Bharali Cabinet ministers were meeting on the same subject. The foreign minister was reporting the rumours his ambassador was picking up in Ottawa.

'Those Canadians are crazy,' he said, shaking his head. 'First they pressed hard to win an oil and gas drilling concession. And now they want the embassy to pull up stakes? Must be some form of national mental disorder from lack of sunshine. Or maybe head injuries on hockey rinks. In any event, Canada by itself is too small to matter but if other countries follow their lead, we could get isolated. Something must be done.'

The King stroked his mustache thoughtfully. 'I think we must help guide them to the right decision. Do you remember what we did when the Americans wanted to close their military base?'

'Ah, yes,' replied the foreign minister. 'The Airbase gambit. Brilliant. I'll start right away.'

C3 C3 C3 CB

It all began quietly: a small remark by the Bharali Ambassador at a reception on Parliament Hill hosted by George Crowley himself.

'Minister,' said the ambassador, seemingly by chance, 'There are unfortunate rumours circulating about my country. I want you to believe me. Bharalya is *not* developing weapons of mass destruction, despite what some are saying.'

The minister almost choked on his cocktail olive. 'What do you mean "weapons of mass destruction"?'

'Oh, the usual. Biological weapons, small nuclear devices, that sort of thing. Those tunnels and underground laboratories are only being used for peaceful purposes. You have nothing to worry about, Minister.'

The minister took his chief of staff into an alcove as soon as he could escape the party. 'Where there's smoke, there's fire,' he whispered, clearly disturbed. 'Find out more, and fast.'

An urgent request to Percy produced a TOP SECRET report the next morning:

> *'There have indeed been rumours of unusual activity in the mountains lately. We have no intelligence, however, to believe it is related to military purposes. At least, not yet.*

'That damned ambassador is using weasel words again,' fumed the minister. 'I think he knows something. Get Public Security and CSIS on this right away. The last thing we need just now is another international security crisis.'

Two days later, Willy, Crowley's chief of staff, ran into the office waving yet another report from Percy. 'Normally, I wouldn't bother you with these routine country assessments, Minister, but I think you'd better look at this one. It's Bharalya again. Something's up.'

The minister took one look at the title and swallowed hard: *Bharalya: A Future Haven for Terrorists?'* The minister got so red in the face his chief of staff asked him if he was feeling all right. 'Get the Minister of Public Safety on the phone,' he gasped. 'I think we have a problem.'

Because the minister never read beyond the first few lines of any document, he did not see Percy's conclusion, which stated benignly:

Bharalya is a rock of stability in an unstable region.

The following day, the minister took an urgent call from the Canadian Ambassador to the United Nations in New York. 'Sorry to bother you, sir, but this is important. As you recall, the vote on our candidacy for the Security Council is coming up in a few days. It's going to be close and we've just heard Bharalya is rallying several countries in South and Central Asia to vote in sympathy against Canada.'

'I wasn't aware of that,' said the minister, startled. 'What do you suggest I do?'

'The problem seems to be a rumour that Canada is about to close its embassy and terminate its aid program there, sir. I'm sure it isn't true, but you may want to have a word with Percy Williamson, our ambassador there. I believe he's close to the foreign minister and the king and might be able to help turn the vote around.'

The minister went ballistic. 'Bharalya, Bharalya, Bharalya. That's all I hear about these days. Can't anyone tell me what's going on? Get Percy on the blower as soon as you can.'

Minutes later, an angry minister's voice boomed over the secure phone in Percy's office.

'The United Nations?' Percy asked, sounding surprised. 'I thought you were calling about the kidnapping.'

'What kidnapping?' The minister's throat went dry and his palms began to sweat, as they always did under stress. He popped one of the pills his doctor had prescribed for just such moments.

'Frank Kobayashi, our embassy administrative officer, is missing, sir. He disappeared during the weekend and no one knows where he is. He left no message about where he was going. It's unusual, but you should stay calm for the moment. We have no reason to believe he has been kidnapped by terrorists.'

'Terrorists?' screamed the minister. Alarmed, his chief of staff handed him another pill and refilled his water glass.

'Not to worry, sir. We've contacted the chief of police and he's promised to take charge of the investigation personally. For the moment we recommend you keep this all confidential; a leak could upset the kidnappers—I mean, *alleged* kidnappers—and make future negotiations difficult. I'm sure it will all turn out to be a false alarm but we must treat it seriously. There are terrorist movements all over this region, you know.'

෪෪෪෪

Frank put his feet up on the coffee table and handed his glass to his buddy and drinking companion, Tukman, the Bharali chief of police.

'Don't mind if I do have another wee one. So good of you to invite me, Tukman. I do hope no one's missed me back at the embassy.'

The two of them were doing their best to liquidate the embassy's last remaining case of Johnny Walker Black Label. With Percy's agreement, Frank had thoughtfully liberated it from the embassy cellar and brought it to his friend's summerhouse.

'Actually, Frank, it was my brother-in-law, the foreign minister, who suggested you and I take a few days off. I don't really know why, but he said if we played hooky for a few days, it would help you get that visa to stay on in Bharalya when you retire. I'm supposed to tell no one you're here, including your consul Godfrey.'

'Is he concerned?'

'Well, he called me yesterday morning. I told him I was looking after your "case" personally. And that's exactly what I'm doing. Cheers.'

CECECECE

When the red telephone rang a few days later, Percy was ready.

'Suzanne,' he began, 'what's the latest?'

'Haven't you heard the news, Percy?'

'Not a word,' he said, suppressing a smile.

'Well, Percy, it's amazing. The minister went to Cabinet today but for some strange reason, he didn't propose closing down your embassy after all. In fact, he said the opposite. He made a point of describing Bharalya as a bulwark against international terrorism and an ally at the United Nations. He torpedoed the plans of the Minister for International Cooperation and even pushed through an increase in aid to your country. Apparently, she was none too happy and had a snit-fit right in the Cabinet room.'

'Really?' he replied, the smile now playing on his lips. 'God moves in mysterious ways.'

'Several of his Cabinet colleagues apparently asked him why the change of heart? Do you know what he said?'

'No.'

He said, 'National security. Big-time. Bharalya is critical to Canadian security. That's all I can tell you.'

'Thanks for this, Suzanne. I'll be happy to share the news with the staff.'

He hung up the telephone and sat quietly for a few minutes, savouring the moment. *I think this calls for a celebration,* he decided. *At the government's expense.*

CECECECE

As the champagne was flowing in the embassy boardroom that afternoon, it was also being served in the King's office. Everyone was in a celebratory mood, delighted by the outcome, especially the Bharali foreign minister.

'A toast,' he said, raising his glass, 'to His Majesty.'

'His Majesty,' everyone responded in unison.

'And a toast to Percy Williamson,' replied the King. 'To Percy.'

Everyone cheered and clinked their glasses.

'You know,' the king added with a chuckle, 'I just don't understand Canadian foreign policy. They are very fine people but they have such a knack for snatching defeat from the jaws of victory. This time, they were lucky. Bharalya saved them from themselves.'

'As did Percy, their ambassador,' added the foreign minister. 'His minister will never know how much he helped him do the right thing.'

Epilogue

Embassy life soon returned to normal. In fact, when the summer heat is at its most sizzling, diplomatic life in Bharalya cools to the freezing point. Nothing at all happens. The social calendar is empty, no visitors from Ottawa darken the embassy doorstep, and every diplomat flees for cooler climes. Well, almost every diplomat. Percy had generously given permission to Godfrey, Frank, Piggy, and the Dragon to take the early vacation period this year. He and Sylvie remained behind to keep the embassy functioning until the others returned.

It was a good chance for him to catch up on his light reading. The unexpected knock on his office door almost made him drop the slim volume in his hands, *Esprit de Corps* by Lawrence Durrell. A mop of fiery red hair appeared around the corner, followed by Sylvie's face. Her expression showed something was bothering her. Something serious.

'Ambassador, can I interrupt your reading for a moment? Something has come up which may be important. I need your advice on what to do.'

'Of course, Sylvie,' Percy replied, getting up. They moved to the comfortable leather chairs opposite his desk. 'What's up?'

'Well, I'm not entirely sure, but here's the story. As you know, I worked hard this past year on that oil drilling contract our minister is so keen on.'

'And you did a bang-up job of it too.'

'Thank you. If the Canadian consortium hits oil, and apparently that seems very likely, the shareholders stand to make a lot of money.'

'But not the public servants, of course,' he said to lighten her mood.

'Well, that's the issue, in a way. Last evening I had dinner with the agent who helped the consortium clinch the deal. He let slip some information which quite frankly shocked me.'

'Go on.'

'He said there may be something, well, fishy there.'

'Fishy? In what way?'

'It's all rumours, though. Nothing proven.' And for the next half hour, she told him everything she had heard. As she spoke, his face registered first shock, then anger, and finally, excitement. When she finished, he thanked her profusely. 'Just leave this with me,' he told her. 'I know exactly what to do.'"

Fascinating, absolutely fascinating, he thought to himself after she said good-bye. *Yes, I know what to do.*

CBCBCBCB

A few days after his arrival in Ottawa, Percy stepped jauntily through the doors of the Department of Foreign Affairs on Sussex Drive and walked directly into the elevator to the executive floor. He was sporting a natty dark grey pinstripe suit, a bright yellow tie, and mirror-shined Italian black loafers, all brand new for the occasion. *Why not?* he thought. *This is a wonderful day.*

He found himself whistling a happy tune as he emerged at the minister's outer office. 'Ambassador Williamson to see the minister,' he announced cheerfully. 'He's expecting me.' *But not what I have to say,* Percy chuckled to himself.

The receptionist kept him waiting an additional fifteen minutes, as per the minister's instructions, but eventually opened the big oak doors, showed him in, and closed them quietly behind him.

Nothing has changed since our last meeting, Percy thought, as he crossed the football field-sized office. *Except this.*

'Minister,' he said with a radiant smile, 'delighted to see you,' and shook the minister's paw with evident pleasure. He noted that George was flabbergasted by his enthusiasm after all that had happened last year. 'You're probably wondering why I've asked for this private chat with you.'

'As a matter of fact, I am, Percy. It's pretty unusual.'

'It concerns a small but important matter. I need to clear up a detail about that drilling contract you sent me out to Bharalya to win.'

'Perhaps we better sit down then. What about it? It was signed not long ago, wasn't it? It's all done.'

'Maybe, maybe not, Minister.'

With that, the minister's expression changed. He leaned forward, suddenly *very* interested in what Percy was saying. 'Why, is there a problem?'

'That depends on your point of view.'

'What do you mean?'

'Certain, uh, information about the Canadian consortium has recently come to my attention.'

With that, the minister's face hardened. Percy could not be sure if it was anger or fear in his eyes.

'Are you familiar with the CEO of the consortium?'

'Well, yes. I mean, I met him once or twice. Why do you ask?'

'Perhaps over a family dinner?' Percy asked politely. 'Would you by any chance have been invited to that dinner because he is your brother-in-law?'

Silence.

'Well, so what if he is?' the minister finally countered, going on the offensive. 'It's no big deal. I'll admit the Opposition could make some mileage with it if they knew, but we have a majority in Parliament and I can ride it out. So, Percy if that's all …'

He made as if to show Percy the door. To his surprise, Percy did not move. Instead, he sat still, looking thoughtfully at him. Finally, Percy said quietly, 'Minister, do you know what "insider trading" is?'

At that, the minister blanched and reached into a pocket for his pills. He bolted down two with a large glass of water.

'What do you mean?'

'I mean, do you think it is an offence if someone uses privileged information to buy shares in a company before the market has that same information? And make a big profit?'

'That would be a very serious allegation,' he replied, turning away from Percy's unrelenting gaze. 'Anyone making that kind of charge would need to back it up with real proof.'

With that, Percy reached into his briefcase and brought out a large brown envelope. He placed it carefully on the coffee table between them, unopened. He sat back and looked the minister in the eye again. The two men stayed silent for several more minutes.

It was the minister who blinked first.

'Percy,' he said, 'I don't know what you're talking about but while you've been speaking, I've been thinking about that World Bank job you talked to me about almost a year ago. You know, I believe you *would* be a good fit there. Are you still interested? I can speak to the Prime Minister personally about it this afternoon. I'm sure we can have all the arrangements made within, say, two weeks. Would that be acceptable?'

Percy said nothing for a few seconds. Then he smiled and replied, 'Yes, Minister. That would be quite acceptable.'

The minister then reached for the envelope. Percy wagged a finger and said, 'No, Minister, I think I'll hold on to this for the moment. If you don't mind.'

He retrieved the incriminating envelope, closed his briefcase and strolled to the door without even saying good-bye. A clearly worried minister remained alone in his office, thinking.

CBCBCBCB

That evening, Percy and Marilyn were seated in the plush, candlelit dining room of the rooftop restaurant at their hotel. She was elegant in a simple black dress with her trademark silver pearls. The smile in her eyes danced in the flickering candlelight. Bharalya seemed far away as they clinked their glasses and toasted their future.

'Percy,' she was saying, 'we've been talking for hours but you still haven't answered the big question.'

'Which is?'

'What on earth was in the envelope?"

'The envelope? Oh, the breakfast menu from the hotel. It was just the right size.'